The Bandit's Adventure

By: Katrina Hawkins

Published by Katrina Hawkins
United States of America
ISBN: 9798370085208
Hardcover ISBN: 9798370085024

Dedication

To my family who always give me great ideas or give me inspiration to create strong independent characters who try to protect what they love and work hard.

~Trina

Contents

There are those in the government and those that are not. Some are called bandits or pirates, others army or navy. The world had large continents, three to be exact, at least in the known world. Many had never tried to sail around the continents since the nations on those large places were at war and to land in the wrong place could result in death. Even those that were in an alliance and created Naval fleets had no idea. The navy was used to escort merchants across from the big continents or to the smaller ones.

Many who traveled and ate from the wild fruits found that they developed powers, being blessed by the world as a traveler and lover of the land. The Navy took recruits out on training expeditions specifically for them to develop those powers during their boot camp. Everyone developed differently from the same fruits and some found that if they only ate the vegetation then they would develop completely different types of powers.

The sea was a kill or be killed kind of place. Which most young recruits were used to if they lived near the border to a different territory or kingdom, it was second nature for those that had fought before. Some recruits from peaceful villages were in for a rude awakening.

Saber grew up in a village on the border between Lidsing and Ruld, it was the most ruthless and lawless village for both kingdoms considering it was on the border and neither kingdom held it long enough to protect its citizens. Most were bandits or military families and there were fights every day in the streets. Kids and women who lived there fought just as often as the men outside the village. Saber was the youngest daughter in an otherwise all male house, her mother died long before she was even named. Her family were bandits and before Saber was very old, she was well aware that there had to be more to life than fighting. Her father refused to hear it...until her brothers were all wiped out in a fight. Saber had been ambushed in the village the same day but had evaded the attack. They mourned that night but Saul Barca, Saber's father, told her to leave.

"Where am I going?"

"Anywhere but here," Saul didn't look at her as he ate his soup that she cooked for him, "Go find out for yourself if there is more to life than fighting. I won't last much longer anyway so instead of risking the bandits falling apart and our families being completely massacred when we are detained...go."

Saber nodded once and started to travel, she knew from living in the village it was better to dress like a man so no one would hit on you. She was nearly 13 but seemed older to most men it seemed. She kept her sword close as she traveled but everywhere she went she nearly starved. She stayed in Ruld since that was the kingdom who never attacked her village. She didn't have money for food so hunted and survived in the wilderness. Everywhere she looked she found poverty and more fighting. The separation of social classes made it hard on the people it seemed.

Saber was caught in the capital of Ruld for pickpocketing and instead of a jail sentence as well as the fact that this was her first infraction, they ordered her to attend a correctional school. It was actually the judge's family taking her in and forcing her to learn to read and write. At that point in her life, she had never found a use to learn letters or read. She tried to be good but local kids around their house picked on her for being a backwoods idiot. Saber ignored it until it came to blows, then she dominated everyone. The judge yelled often about her getting into trouble but she didn't argue or say anything about it.

"Why do you do that?" he demanded, "These are military families and it's a peaceful little part of town, Saber."

"It's my business old man, butt out," she growled but he always lectured her and disciplined her for that answer. Until one day a soldier caught the fight and had witnessed it from the beginning. She was attacked first and outnumbered four to one. They got the first few punches in but she knocked them all for a loop. The judge asked her again and she glared at him giving her signature response, "My business, butt out old man."

He tried to get her to cave and tell him the truth but she wouldn't. His wife asked Saber to come sit with her and asked about where she was from, to tell a story or any local legends. Saber wasn't having it, she had successfully not told them anything about her home town and she wouldn't.

Four months into the living arrangement and Saber had a high fever from an injury that she didn't tell them about that became infected. She called out to her brothers and her pa, the judge's wife, Giselle, called a doctor to come see to her. He checked her for any wounds and found plenty of scars and the infected wound. He treated her and looked to the judge, "Where did you find this girl, judge?"

"Here in the capital, why?" Judge Ulric Thompson frowned.

"She's not from here, she's from the borderlands," the doctor told him, "See this mark?"

"Ruld North Bandits, I thought the RNB were wiped out by Lidsing a few months ago," Giselle asked in shock.

"They were, the entire RNB village after two weeks of fighting," the doctor murmured, "From these scars she's seen a ton of fighting in her life and survived against the odds time and time again."

Saber coughed and started to wake up, she was thirteen at the time and found their worried faces staring at her, "Who's this?"

"Doctor Henric for your fever," Ulric sighed, "How do you feel?"

"Fine, old man, I don't need no doctor."

"Saber," Giselle warned, she was a language fiend when it came to grammar and use of words. Saber had learned a lot over the months but her language when she was tired or, as in this case, injured made it impossible to remember.

"Get some rest," Ulric murmured, "You have an infection from an injury it seems."

It had been a bad fight and Saber had been lucky to avoid really bad injuries, some older kids were picking on the younger ones and she stopped them—although she didn't want a fight. Saber took a breath but Ulric raised his hand and stalled her out with a 'we will talk when your fever is gone.'

He had told her that he would send her to a detention center if she didn't quit fighting and she didn't like the sounds of this center. She had no idea what that meant but she didn't want anything to do with it.

When she healed, Ulric seemed to have forgotten and the subject was never raised. Saber traveled with them when Ulric had to travel to judge bandits or pirates. Saber heard the news about her old village but no tears came when Giselle brought it up in passing when another village with another bandit group was wiped off the border by Ruld this time. Saber froze for a second and asked, "They killed everyone, even the women and children?"

"Yes, just like the RNB village. Not a soul survived from what the military reported although some could have vanished in the night before the attack, who knows."

Saber knew her father wouldn't vanish, if there was a fight he never backed down or ran away. That was how Saber was taught as well.

Months passed; Saber finally gave in to tell Giselle her birthday when she turned 14. They were in a port city at the time and Giselle asked if she wanted to shop for new clothes since she had another growth spurt again. Saber shrugged and walked with her down the streets of the port town. Saber always had her guard up since the older children liked to surprise attack in the capital and she was used to living in the bandit world of always be cautious or you die motto. New cities were no different, especially when Giselle and her were alone, she felt the need to protect Giselle.

They shopped at two shops and started heading back to the military hotel they were staying at. Saber held the bags in one hand and walked with Giselle looking at the ocean in surprise, "It's so blue."

"It is," Giselle smiled, "Have you ever seen the ocean before?"

"No," Saber shook her head.

"Let's go stick our feet in the water," Giselle chuckled and they went to the water's edge and stuck their feet in. Saber noticed they had rubberneckers watching from different places but didn't confront them. That was until three burly men walked toward them and smiled lazily at the water's edge. Their shoes were where the men were standing but Saber and Giselle had kept the bags in their hands. Saber straightened instantly and handed over the bags and told Giselle, "Don't say a word, auntie."

Giselle was auntie because she acted like a favorite aunt while the judge was more of an annoying family member who nagged too much. Saber was attached to them by this point and would protect Giselle even if it meant getting thrown to some center. She didn't deserve their kindness anyway, if they knew her past they would throw her away like unwanted trash and she didn't want to see that happen.

"Saber," Giselle started but Saber met her eyes.

Maybe she had a look in her eyes or maybe Giselle was surprised to see a reassuring smile but Giselle didn't say anything more. Saber moved out of the water although she stayed on the firmer sand where the water lapped at it. She looked at the three and said, "Is there a problem?"

"Give us all your cash and there won't be," the middle one said.

"Nah I kinda like the broad, she's older but still a looker," the one on the right said.

"I'll give you one chance to scram, she is Judge Thompson's wife and the military really don't like their women messed with," Saber met his gaze, her hands were on her hips studying them.

"Judge Thompson's wife?" the one on the far left murmured surprised, "Listen guys, I know that old dog and he's no joke. He was known as the scorpion in his military days in the army."

"Who cares?" the one on the right frowned, "I just want a little fun."

"Saber," Giselle started but Saber shook her head slightly without turning around.

"Auntie stay put," Saber murmured as the three started toward her. Saber took one out that was wanting to run, she attacked fast and pulled his sword as he fell, the dagger she kept hidden in the waistband of her pants was in her non-dominant hand.

"Ohhhh I'm so scared," the one who wanted to have some fun with Giselle crooned as if this was a game. The one in the middle frowned instantly looking to the one on the ground.

"Matteo get up."

"Damn she has a mean hook," the one she attacked first, Matteo grumbled, "Let's just go Lee. It's not worth it."

"I'm not going until we teach her what her place is," the pervert growled.

"Justice leave it alone," Matteo complained.

"No," the pervert, Justice, shook his head.

Saber dodged a surprise attack from Justice and caught the blade that Lee lounged with. She was fighting grown men and standing her ground although she was taking injuries fast. Matteo didn't join in; he wanted no part in it although they had a crowd and Giselle had yelled for someone to call the Navy. Saber trembled and blood was mucking up her grip on the sword. She surprised Justice with lounging, his sword ricocheted off her own and cut her arm hard as her sword went into his chest. She didn't waste time trying to get it out, seeing Lee moving in with a yell. Saber let go of the sword and jumped back from Lee's attack.

His attacks had a long reach and she was in for a fight for her life with just a knife. Saber risked a glance toward Justice and found he was plucking at the sword, it was fatal and he had fallen to the sand, and Lee was ticked. Matteo had moved to Justice not sure how to help but not focused on Giselle at least.

Saber ducked and skid in the sand, at one point crab crawling away from him as he attacked her. Suddenly three men tackled him to the ground and she quickly looked for Giselle, finding Navy had surrounded the entire scene and Giselle met her eyes. Saber was breathing fast and heard a voice she wished hadn't shown up, not even noticing she flinched at the tone of voice he had used—it was like her dad's military voice—all business. Happy Birthday, Saber thought to herself.

She struggled to her feet, feeling the burn from the water and sand in every cut and scrap. She turned to look at Ulric, swiping blood out of her left eye, "Well Old Man, I guess now you get to throw me away to whatever center you mentioned. It...it was nice while it lasted."

"What are you talking about, Saber," Ulric frowned at her, Giselle in his arms. Tears swimming in her eyes she met his gaze.

"You said if I fought, you'd send me away...but Auntie was in trouble," Saber shook, the stress hitting hard and her wavering on her feet. A soldier came from her left to take her knife and she reacted on instinct, defensively holding the knife and facing whoever came from her blind spot since the blood had glued her eye shut. The soldier raised his hands.

"Easy, that's evidence now, kid," he murmured.

Saber frowned not understanding, "It's mine, how am I supposed to survive without at least this? It's not like the Old Man had let me keep my sword."

"Saber," Ulric stepped toward her, taking it from her and giving it to the man, "You became chatty it seems."

"I guess near death experiences make me speak my mind," Saber retorted, it was true since her brothers always complained she verbally assaulted them more after a fight than any other time.

"Let the medic check you out," Ulric guided her toward the medic on site.

"The doctor took the one to the hospital for surgery," the medic murmured.

"He's lucky to be alive at all," another guy in a Navy uniform growled.

"It'll be a miracle if he lives," another commented as the medic looked Saber over. Tears streaked down her face, she couldn't stop shaking and Giselle touched her hair gently.

"What were you thinking, Saber? You could've been killed!"

"They would've hurt you," Saber shook her head looking up through her tears angrily at Giselle—did she think the world was perfect and she was safe? "They wouldn't have stopped with just the money. The pervert said he wanted to have fun with you. I tried to warn them off but they wouldn't...they wouldn't listen. I wasn't going to let it happen."

"Saber you—"

"Over my dead body," Saber growled through her teeth, her eyes shown with a fire Giselle didn't understand, "There weren't any Navy on the beach, Auntie. The only way to live is to watch your own back and those that you care about. I won't regret it and I won't apologize! It's done, drop it."

Giselle stared in surprise to see Saber's eyes were glacier cold and tears were still streaming down her face. Ulric took a breath but the medic beat him to it.

"You are going to have a scar but I don't think you need surgery. You are one lucky girl."

Saber was silent as he cleaned her up and treated every cut and scrap. She stood unsteadily and walked to the water's edge for her sandals. She was still shaking and it wouldn't stop. Giselle caught her arm and Ulric grabbed their bags, "Let's head to the hotel."

"Ulric she's shaking," Giselle looked to him.

"Saber," Ulric met her eyes, tears were still falling and he knew she didn't cry easily.

"I won't fight you, Old Man, a deal's a deal after all," Saber looked at the sand seemed to shrink into herself for a second.

"Saber what are you talking about?" Giselle asked confused.

Saber stood straight, wincing at bruises and cuts but didn't say another word. Ulric watched as the trembling slowed and her tears dried up before they even took three steps. He noticed a large crowd and some looked like friends of the three that attacked them. Saber shrugged off Giselle's worried hand and walked confidently toward the carriage waiting for them, her arm bandage red as well as some other bandages already turning red. Ulric didn't see her eyes shuttling through the crowd or that she identified four men who seemed angry or upset who were probably friends with those people.

Ulric took her to the Navy to answer any questions they had, she answered them since Ulric was harassing her into answers. When a Navy Officer asked why she seemed so upset having been told she could fight and when pressed Saber simply said, "Fighting where I'm from is live or die. It's just been a while since I had a close shave."

"What do you mean?"

Saber studied him in silence, if she said more then Ulric really would send her away. Saber looked away and Ulric told the officer it wasn't vital to his investigation. Giselle was escorted to the hotel and protected by a squad as they questioned Saber. When they were nearly done around supper time there was a tap at the door and a messenger announced that the man had died from his injuries. Saber tensed, yes she had killed before but not a grown man and not in front of people who would haul her off to prison.

Ulric hadn't turned toward the door but was still staring at Saber so seen the small jerk before she froze as if being still meant they wouldn't notice her. Ulric sighed softly, "We will continue this discussion tomorrow. Saber is still underage and it was self-defense. Admiral, may I take her to the hotel?"

"Yes," the Admiral looked to Saber, catching her eyes and said, "Don't try to run away or we may have to re-evaluate your situation, understand?"

"Yes sir," Saber kept her face deadpan, she could outrun them and hide but...was it worth the effort? If she did that what would happen to Giselle and the Old Man? If she went to prison she wouldn't be able to answer the question deep in her heart she wanted to know most. The question she wanted answered was still proving to be yes but with the ocean she realized there was more to the world than this specific country. If she tried to escape, she wanted to go to the ocean and see new lands and cultures. Ulric murmured, "Let's go, Saber."

They rode a carriage to the hotel; a naval squad was protecting them and Saber felt naked without her knife. Ulric studied her, seeing her fists in her lap as she looked toward the door although the carriage windows were shuttered and no one could see in or out. He sighed and murmured, "You have said a few times this afternoon that I will 'throw you away' to a center for fighting."

Saber winced as she closed her eyes, waiting for him to continue but he didn't say another word. "I don't know what the center is but...I don't want to leave Auntie...or you, Old Man. You said not to fight but I've seen men like them before and I knew if I didn't stall them or at least try to fight them off that Auntie would have been injured and maybe even killed. I didn't want that to happen...even though it went against my promise not to fight anymore."

"Saber, let me clarify a few things. First of all there are different types of fights. Do you know what I mean by that?"

"Those you start and those you finish?" she cocked her head feeling tired from all the anxiety.

"There is that but mostly it's meaningless ones for different purposes or ones where you are defending yourself and others. Ones that you can and should walk away from and ones where it's critical to fight to protect yourself or another individual. When I told you to not fight I meant not to jump into a fight that you could walk away from. This fight today was one where you meant to protect yourself and Giselle, one that I doubt you could have walked away from without a fight. Those types of fights, although dangerous are not ones that I would send you to a detention center for, Saber. There might be some repercussions but it's doubtful. There were so many witnesses that we have bystanders and off duty navy guards reporting what they saw and heard."

"You won't send me away?" Saber looked to him, just maybe she could hope to stay a little longer. Her eyes started to pool and she couldn't seem to get her emotions in check for the day.

"No, Giselle would kill me if I did. She's attached to you like a daughter….Saber when you were injured a few months back and feverish due to an infected cut. I didn't say anything because I heard you were defending someone else…and I didn't want you to worry."

"I never brought it up," Saber looked at the window, waiting for him to continue.

"I know you are from the RNB village, Saber," he murmured softly.

Saber grit her teeth tight to keep from responding in surprise, he didn't need to know that! "How?"

"The doctor had to search for the injury, we found the tattoo on your back."

"What now, Old Man?" Saber frowned.

"Tell me everything, Saber, we aren't sure what happened up there and the Army wants to know what is happening and if there were any survivors who had escaped the massacre. I haven't told them about you but I would like a little more information."

"Why?"

"Because although they were bandits, they have always fought to keep the border their territory. With the enemy targeting the bandits and wiping them out we aren't sure what they plan. Although we have targeted those bandits that align with Lidsing. I have never been to RNB so I'm curious about them."

"Nothing I say will get me in trouble?" Saber met his gaze feeling exhausted, to the point that she would speak her mind.

"Nothing you say will be used against you, Saber," he sighed.

"Sixty years ago the RNB was an Army post nicknamed Rumble because they were always fighting. My grandpa was the commander of the post. The Army was tired of having to replace fighters and protecting that specific part due to the bad weather and terrain. It was difficult to defend because of the cliffs and valleys around the village. They were ordered to fall back to the fort about three miles back from the border. My grandpa and his men refused, it would give in to the enemy and although it was difficult to defend it would give the enemy a bridgehead. The Army knew the place so well it was easier on our men and the enemy ended up killing themselves trying to get to the location. His men all resigned from the Army and my grandpa continued to lead them. It was a village so the women and children were all there. It was a rough post, sometimes military spouses were required to fight as well because of the attacks. When the Army left, their supply of food and supplies, suddenly my grandpa had to figure out how to keep their people alive. They took from any who attacked and although they tried to pay for supplies when they traveled to the other villages, there were harsh times when they couldn't so they'd steal from the enemy villages—gaining the title of bandits although they avoided Ruld unless necessary. I had four older brothers; three that I remember, and one that was stolen in a Lidsing raid just before my birth.

"My brothers were protective and taught me everything they knew about fighting. They never pulled their punches, everyone knew the Rumble motto—fight or die—there was no between and it didn't matter your age, you trained from the time you started to walk. I dressed in breeches and large shirts so no one could see I was a girl in case of attack. Before you ask, my dad was still alive when I left the town...my mom died shortly after my birth from complications. We fought for our lives, I...I was seven when I killed for the first time. A teenage scout attacked the kids near the river and I was the oldest among them and tasked with protecting them. You had to grow up fast or die young."

Saber didn't know the Navy were outside the carriage listening in horror at what a young girl had went through in the mountains as they escorted them to the hotel. Ulric murmured, "Your brothers? Did they leave with you?"

"Half the village was killed during the first week of attacks...my brothers passed the night my father told me to run. He told all the young to run away but to make sure we went in all different directions and not more than two together. Families were going together but I left in the dead of night alone, I have no idea how many actually survived. Ex-communication...if you see someone from the village you avoid them and pretend you don't know them. That's the orders my father gave to me when I left. I traveled for a few months and survived in the woods. I want to know if there is more to life than fighting, my father said to find out for myself and to travel. I visited different places and you know what happened when I hit the capital, you can't hunt and fish in a big city so I was picking pockets when I was caught and my sword was taken by the army there."

"I see...Giselle wants to eat supper at a restaurant, don't worry about getting out of the carriage, she will be joining us soon," Ulric murmured when the carriage stopped, "So you are staying with us because you were caught...I don't understand why you didn't run away but I'm more curious to why every time Giselle asks what you want to do when you grow up you avoid the question. Why is that?"

"All I know is fighting, Old Man, I don't know how to be a girlie girl and I don't think auntie will understand me at all if I tried to explain to her my history," Saber grumbled opening the window and seeing Giselle coming out to join them.

"Did you have fun shopping at least?" Ulric asked knowing from her look that they were out of time to talk seriously. Giselle had always been sheltered although she understood Ulric fought in wars and even as a judge there was some danger to his life. She was from nobility so didn't fully grasp it although she loved Saber like a daughter and knew that being from a bandit group meant she had a rough life.

"It's different, Auntie Giselle forced at least three dresses into those bags even though I said I wouldn't wear them," Saber muttered as a Naval guard opened the door and helped Giselle in.

"I heard that, Saber," Giselle chuckled.

"I don't like dresses, they get your legs tangled when you need them most," Saber grumbled.

Ulric chuckled at that. Giselle shook her head as Saber leaned against the window looking out the window, "When are we leaving this place? I think I've overstayed my welcome."

"Probably right," Ulric murmured, "I believe one more day, Saber."

"Okay," Saber sighed.

"So, if today's your birthday, how did your parents settle on such an unusual name as Saber?" Giselle shocked the two sitting with her as well as the squad outside the carriage eavesdropping.

Saber looked to Ulric who gave a micro-nod that she knew where Saber was from it seemed, "My mother passed a few days after I was born but she was comatose since my birth. My father asked my brothers what they wanted to name me since that was what they wanted to do. They argued over which weapons were the best...I'm just glad Saber is the one that won out. I didn't ask what was in the running, I was a little worried I wouldn't like their naming choices."

"True there are a lot of weapons in the world and not all of them would make good names for a little girl," Ulric mused to himself.

"So that's how I got Saber. My full name is Saber Aldara Barca, a mouthful so I always just go by Saber."

"What does Aldara mean?" Giselle asked fully invested and loving that Saber was now opening up. She didn't realize it was exhaustion, mental fatigue that made Saber answer them without hesitation.

"It's Old Ruld meaning caution in battle. My family always prepared to fight with our father saying Aldara meaning to use your head and don't act rashly."

"Barca...isn't that the war hero's surname from the war nearly seventy years back?" Giselle frowned looking to Ulric thoughtfully.

"It was, he was a great tactician and they placed him in the most difficult commands because he always found a solution," Ulric murmured looking at Saber who looked out the window again.

"Where are we headed, auntie?" Saber asked curious since they were still riding through town.

"Ulric and I always come to this particular restaurant when we visit the port. It has the best seafood. You haven't eaten seafood before, have you?"

"Like fish and stuff?" Saber asked confused.

"And stuff," Ulric smirked, "It's from the ocean. Fishermen go out into the ocean and pull up all kinds of different fish and bring it back to the market in port or to the restaurants."

Saber spent the rest of the evening trying different seafood and finding she loved it. The navy squad assigned to their protection was shocked when the staff brought out a cake for her birthday and she froze in surprise. "What is this?"

"Haven't you had a birthday cake before?" Giselle asked amused.

"No," Saber was beyond tired and Ulric could see it as she stifled yawns continuously.

"Oh, well traditionally when you have a birthday you get cake and receive presents from people. Although you didn't tell us until today that it was your birthday so we didn't go overboard on gifts."

"Gifts for what?" Saber was confused.

"To celebrate another year," Giselle looked to Ulric for help explaining.

"It's something most children in the country are used to, Saber, every year to mark a birthday you would get presents from family and friends and eat cake to celebrate the day you were born into the world."

"But...it's just another day," Saber was confused but Giselle shook her head.

"Not anymore it isn't," Giselle pulled out a gift wrapped in parchment paper and Saber looked at it. She had never unwrapped a gift before. If they got someone something it was usually a weapon and was just handed to them, this was new territory for her. She looked to Ulric and Giselle both watching her expectantly. Saber cocked her head.

"What does it do?" Saber asked confused, "Do I have to write stuff on it to learn more words with auntie?"

Ulric laughed as Giselle's jaw dropped in shock. Everyone was watching them, unsure why the girl with bandages was looking at a gift like it was foreign to her. Ulric still chuckling told her to tear off the parchment paper. She knew paper was expensive in villages like her hometown so she carefully undone the paper without tearing it and looked at the box. She opened it to find a necklace with Giselle's family crest on it. She looked to Giselle in surprise, it matched Giselle's necklace exactly, "It's really mine?"

"You are a part of this family," Ulric met her gaze, "Hopefully we can break some more of your bad habits but until you are considered an adult, we would like you to stay with us...as our daughter."

"Are you serious, Old Man?" Saber whispered in disbelief.

"I'm serious," Ulric chuckled, "But stop calling me that."

Saber paused to meet his eyes, "That might be impossible since I always call you that."

"Well try, I'm not that old!"

Saber smirked and Giselle watched as Ulric came around to her seat to put the necklace on her, touching her head gently, "My gift will come when we get back to the house at the capital, Saber."

"This is more than enough; I didn't expect anything and this is way more than a gift."

"Let's try the cake," Giselle smiled as the staff sang to her, along with Giselle who had a pretty voice. Saber was shocked and barely kept the tears at bay although it was a close call. She fell asleep before they even got to the hotel, her exhaustion was so much that Ulric carried her up to their suite of rooms they all shared. The squad of navy stared as he gently picked her up and she mumbled something in her sleep. Ulric heard a name but didn't recognize it.

After that day, Ulric trained Saber how to fight, surprised at how much she knew and even hired trainers if she was interested in something specific. Giselle continued to educate her and by the time she turned seventeen she was educated and lethal. As the years passed, she asked Ulric if she could join the navy, she had learned that they protected other ships from pirates and travelled all over the known world. She wanted to answer the question if there were more to life than fighting. She fought to protect from bullies but everyone knew about her and if she appeared they ran, afraid of her by then since she was stronger than any of them. Ulric and Giselle were both well aware of her thirst to find that answer. Ulric knew she would need to know how to protect herself and what better way than to push her knowledge by training. They bonded and she even considered him like a father figure since her own was gone. Many in the military realm knew about the adopted daughter Ulric had and that she was interested in the Navy.

Not many women entered the Navy but they were allowed. So at 17 she was about to enter the Navy and go through their bootcamp. Ulric and

Giselle moved closer to the port city where she would train and during the off hours where she didn't have anything to do she would go to their house for a meal and talk. Ulric asked how it was going and she complained that she was bored, too easy.

She didn't realize an Admiral was visiting for supper as she took off her boots at the door and pulled her hair out of the standard bun they were supposed to wear for training. "I could do it in my sleep. They announce where we are going tomorrow."

"Which ship would you want to go on?" Giselle asked amused as she walked in her stocking feet into the dining room with a stretch.

"As long as I'm not stuck with the noble brats who have whined the whole training, I'm fine with anywhere. Although I don't think I'd fit in with the strait-laced crews."

"Bad luck then," the Admiral smirked, "You were assigned to my ship."

"Old man, did you pull strings for this?" Saber's eyes had a habit of turning icy when she was angry and the Admiral looked surprised.

"I...Why are you upset?" Giselle asked looking near tears.

"No reason," Saber shut down her argument since Giselle was upset. Ulric and Saber both knew why it wasn't a good idea but it seemed Giselle had been the one to pull strings without telling Ulric about it either since he seemed just as surprised. The Admiral smirked amused.

"Don't worry, you will have fun with a straight-laced crew."

So starts Saber's adventure.

Chapter 1

Saber cleaned the ship from top to bottom, as a new recruit to the navy she had to earn her keep. She wore the standard belt knife and sword since they dealt with pirates but she never used it in the three months they had been out on the ocean. Crew members were separated by gender so the three females on the Admiral's ship stayed in a large room in the center of the ship in hammocks strung across the room. The men were just below their room. Saber was quiet and only did what was ordered. The Admiral kept her busy as they traveled their section of ocean water. He was well aware of her history since Ulric was a friend and he had met her on multiple occasions, one included questioning her after the attack at the beach when she was 14 years old against three grown men, although she hadn't recognized him.

As the Admiral of the fleet, they didn't escort merchant ships, they patrolled near the Ruld coast to make sure pirates didn't raid the kingdom. On calm days they all took turns sparing. Saber was one of the top contenders on the crew although she was the youngest. The first mate had just thrown her head over heels and followed up with a lounge but Saber dodged although she had been winded by the violent throw.

"Good!" he growled continuing to keep her on the defensive. Saber couldn't win against him and had never went up against the Admiral but everyone else had lost to her.

"Black Flag!" the crow's nest announced surprising everyone. Saber put the wooden sword away as the first mate told her to stay ready, she was going to get her feet wet since she was finally used to the pitching of the deck and could hold her own. Another call before they could even see the pirate's ship, "Merchant and Fleet ship running ahead of the pirate! Looks as though they have both sustained damage. Mast damage to the fleet ship, one more blow and it's over for them."

"Three ships, one a pirate," the first mate mused looking up at the nest.

"Let's see how they fair against all of us," the Admiral had stepped out of his room and they all went to work changing direction to head toward the ships. Saber knew the drill of getting to a pirate ship, she had her job down pat. She also knew that no person on the ship had any of their crazy 'gifts' since they were mostly nobility. Even during training, she was surrounded by nobles so they didn't even go out to eat the fruit or vegetables to gain powers. Not that Saber wanted or needed them. She finished the preparations and noticed the pirates didn't change course, if the Admiral was coming, she would have ran. Something wasn't right but she didn't have time to ponder it since they were getting information about each ship as they prepared. They had to avoid the fleet ship as well as the merchant since their masts had both taken damage and could fall at any time.

"Very well, let's spring their trap in whatever way we can," the Admiral murmured, Saber knew something was wrong but she never thought it could be a trap, she was standing at her station to relay orders to the crew below for the Admiral and she looked up at him.

"A trap? How do you mean, sir?"

"A pirate attacks and others are waiting in the wings just out of sight of the crow's nest to wait until whatever help comes to assist and attacks when our focus is on the one pirate in front of us. It is a tactic that is old but very productive for them. I don't think they know it's my ship just yet or they may try to run, however if they do know it's ours then we could have a large scale attack headed our way. Keep your head on a swivel when you aren't relaying orders, Saber, understand?"

"Yes sir," she nodded.

They had come to approve and appreciated her fighting skills in practice and from the training camp she was the highest ranked recruit. Knowing her background the Admiral trusted her gut instincts since she was a veteran when it came to fighting.

They prepared for the fight, as they attacked the pirate ship, Saber looked around for a moment as she finished yelling to reload the cannons. There were over two hundred men on the ship, the fleet ship didn't try to turn to help, they were escorting the merchant ship directly to the coast.

"Saber, call for backup from the port. I hope we can last."

"What?" Saber froze following his dark gaze to the horizon. Six pirate ships, although small they would be overwhelmed, "Ah right!"

She ran to the Admiral's quarters and summoned help. One crew always answered the call and their captain reminded her of her family. They were considered the Navy Pirates because they were wild and barely ever followed the laws. Saber liked them, when she got on the long-range communications device she hit the button to show their location, "What's wrong Saber, you sound tense."

"Captain Hank, first it looked like three ships, a merchant, a fleet ship, and a pirate. We engaged and now we have six more pirate ships heading toward us."

"We'll be there in an hour, hold out until then," he murmured.

"Yes sir," she agreed, other Captains of the fleet responded similarly since it was a summons for help. Saber had confirmed four captains before she was summoned back, she raced back to her post, "Captain Hank and three others confirmed sir."

"Good," Admiral murmured, "Let's take care of this ship before the other six get here. Fire at the target on the port side. Once that's done, we are closing with our enemy. Prepare yourself, I need you to fight like our lives depend on it."

"Yes sir," she yelled orders quickly and cannons fired fast. They positioned themselves with the pirate ship between them and the other six. When they closed, Saber shocked her crew as she was at the front with the first mate. He growled, "Don't die, kid, I put time into you and you still have some to learn from me."

"Yes sir," she grinned pulling her knife as well and settling on the balls of her feet. The crew were shocked to see her smiling.

The pirates were equally surprised but because she was smiling a few targeted her. She was like a tornado, she didn't have to worry about repercussions as she did when she was fourteen, she could go full out without worrying about hurting anyone. She targeted tendons and vital points, barely wasting time waiting for them to fall. The fight with the first mate was clean and like a totally different person to those who had seen her fight the crew in the past.

Her and the first mate were so absorbed in the fight that they didn't realize they were barely leaving any for the rest of the crew. The Admiral watched from his post at the helm and cannons sailed toward them. He raised his voice to yell at his crew directing them to the prow where another pirate ship was coming around the one they were fighting. Saber risked a look around to check things out since it was like an intense pressure of anxiety.

"Saber! Go to the stern, there's another heading around," Admiral yelled over the fighting noise.

"I got this kid, get going," the first mate grit his teeth. She pressed forward cutting a path toward the railing and skipped back, three of her crew filled her place and she ran to the stern. She took a deep swig of water and clipped her canteen to her waist again. From the higher position she could see that some of the ships got onto the one they were fighting and were trying to surge forward. The Admiral glanced back at her and said, "We have a while to hold out, I'm leaving the stern in your command, I will focus on the other sides. Dewayne and George's teams are yours, Saber."

"Yes sir," she frowned, he gave her the two teams she knew the best and they had served with Hank in the past so were a little rougher around the edges than the others. She looked at the ship coming around to them as Haven bandaged her arm, "I'm setting up in the sick bay, send anyone down there that needs it...if they can make it."

"Thanks Haven," Saber smiled reassuringly toward her, "I'm sure we will be fine."

"What's the plan, Saber?" George asked curiously.

"We have the higher ground, get some poles, they will have to climb up or swing from their masts. Assign three people spaced to reach the entire back of the ship. The rest prepare to rotate if one of them are injured."

What do you mean we are just defending?" Dewayne growled angrily.

"Hey," she turned to him and frowned, "Let's see what they do first. Send an order to the cannons in the stern, tell them to aim as far down as they can toward the waterline. If they have to bail water out they won't be interested in fighting. Most pirates don't know how to swim so let's make them sweat. If we have any guns that would cause a lot of damage then do the same from up here. Hit these two ships and see if that gets any reaction."

"Devious," Dewayne grinned happily turning to his team. Time seemed to always slow when there was fighting but she heard a yell from the Admiral's room where Brooklyn was stationed to update their summoned aid.

"Ten minutes until reinforcements come!" she called up to the Admiral.

"Hear that, Saber?" he asked loudly.

"Just tell me when you see them!" she growled fighting off another pirate who swung from their mast over to attack them and he was proving to be a good fighter, "George keep your head on a swivel, I'm busy!"

"Aye!" he called.

"Pay attention, naval wench!" the pirate swiped and she ignored the searing pain in her cheek where he had barely sliced her face.

She let loose again, she knew she was getting tired, blood was dripping onto her white uniform and her hat was missing so the sun was blazing in her eyes any time she looked toward the horizon for more enemies that could be there. She pulled a fancy move her brother taught her, he called it spinning top, dropping to the ground to swipe their feet, while one hand cut their thigh as they jumped. She used the sword and instead of swiping she used the momentum to use her knife to bury in his stomach while the spin brought her full circle and back up, swiping across his neck. She grabbed her knife back and let the man drop dead at her feet. She looked around to see George was fighting hard and Dewayne was making fast orders for another wave of enemies.

"Saber! They are in sight!" Brook yelled up at her. She nodded and took a moment to swipe her hands on her pants since blood was making her grip slip again. She yelled at Dewayne who ducked as she attacked the man sneaking up behind him. They were getting pushed back, Will broke his leg when a pirate surprised him with a club.

"Gene and Yancy take Will down to Haven," she ordered stepping between Will and the pirate, "We have to hold our line here, help is coming they are nearly here so keep fighting!"

"Ma'am!" her crewmates growled, they had a loose line of nine facing fifteen pirates. Saber heard a yell from below, "Saber! We hit the pirate ships at the water line."

The pirates heard as well and those in the back turned to look down at the ships, "They aren't lying! We have a massive hole in the prow!"

"Retreat," the pirate who held the club snarled at them. Her group started to step forward to follow after them.

"Hold!" Saber warned her people, "Let them go."

"But!" one guy started but the look she shot him shut him up fast, "Yes ma'am."

"What's your name, Marine wench," the pirate asked.

"You first," she studied him as his friends jumped over the Navy stern toward their own ship.

"The giant Benji," he announced. Saber gave him that, he was taller than any man on their ship and if she had to guess he was around seven and a half feet tall.

"Saber," she watched him.

"Surname or is that your given name?" he cocked his head as he slowly stepped back.

"Barca is my surname," she didn't care if he knew her name.

"I'll remember," he jumped over the edge and Dewayne looked to find all of them were working to save their ship. They turned to retreat and he told Saber as much.

"Any wounded?"

"Cuts and scrapes for our team," George murmured.

"George stay put and secure the stern. Call me if you have more coming," Saber murmured turning and finding the Admiral still giving directions as he fought as well. The first mate was surrounded and they had so many pirates that they were struggling to survive. "Dewayne secure the stairs and have the cannons aim point blank at the pirate on the port side, make sure they hit the deck and don't hurt themselves but cause some mayhem but keep it quiet."

"Yes ma'am," Dewayne nodded, "I'll stay close in case we need to return to assist George."

"Exactly," Saber nodded. Tactical training was coming in handy if it worked for them. Saber raced to attack those giving the Admiral a hard time. She paused as the pirates fell, "I'm heading to the first mate. Our pirates retreated with a hole in the hull at the waterline. I'm leaving George in the stern and Dewayne is having the cannons cause a little trouble for the pirates on the port."

"Go give James a hand," the Admiral nodded. She grabbed a rope and swung over pirates and landed in the circle where the first mate was injured but still holding his own. She smiled as she placed her back to his, "Miss me, sir?"

"What the hell did you come back for, we had enemies in the stern!"

"Taken care of," Saber told him, "They landed with a breach in the hull somehow."

"Really, update me later on how that miraculously happened."

"Brook said help was on the way, can you hold out?" Saber asked politely.

"Don't make me laugh," James growled.

Saber laughed and surprised those in front of her with attacking fast without warning. There was an explosion and the ship was sent rocking wildly but she used the distraction to get another weapon with a longer reach. She threw her knife and locked swords with a pirate taking his sword with another move that was considered cheating when fighting. She had thrown her knife at him as she locked swords, he fell to his knees with the knife in his neck, she made sure he was dead and she had two swords. It was a good thing that Ulric hired someone that wasn't scared to break her arm in training when she was nearly fifteen. It forced her to learn to fight with a sword in her non-dominant hand as well. She liked fighting with two swords although it wasn't customary. She glanced back to find that James was nearly out for the count and she was still surrounded.

A roar came from the other side and everyone looked at that except for the one fighting her. Saber caught his attack and looked as well finding crisp white uniforms storming over the side and swamping the pirates from behind. Saber continued to fight but now they had a wall of other navy forcing the pirates away from them. She turned and helped James to the stairs. He tried to protect but he couldn't even stand on his own. Dewayne took him from her and she turned to look at the situation.

"Saber," Admiral Oliver summoned, she went up and looked around finding that the pirates were now surrounded and unable to retreat.

"So, the ship we fought at the stern was the only one to escape," Saber frowned.

"Seems to be the case, I saw you helping James, how is he?"

"Still wanting to fight," Saber murmured, "Did we injure the ship with attacking with the cannons a few moments ago?"

"Cuts and bruises but no casualties from what Dewayne reported. The pirates on the other hand had a nasty surprise and they have a massive hole in the side of their ship."

"Nice swords, they don't match though," Hank came up with a grin seeing her uniform was red with blood from her enemies as well as herself, her hair had slipped out of the bun and she had a thin cut on her cheek, "We've swarmed the ship so your people can have a small reprieve, Admiral."

"Good," he murmured, "That hour was too long. Saber check on Haven and get a head count of the injured."

"Sir," she slid down the rail and turned into the stairway down into the ship.

They limped back to port to check on the other ship and merchant, six fleet ships arrived to help Saber's crew. No one was unwounded except for Brook and Haven. Saber suffered through getting looked over and when they got into port the Admiral asked Hank's crew if they were interested in going after the ship with the breach in the hull to see if there were any survivors to bring to justice. Hank grinned when he said he was sending Saber with him.

"You noticed which way they were heading so you get to see it through since they hurt your crewmates," Hank told her.

"Twenty-seven of our crew were killed," Saber smirked since her one cheek still hurt and was still bandaged, "I'm happy to be on loan to you, Captain Hank."

His crew were wild and she loved it, it reminded her of family. Admiral Oliver's ship needed repairs so it was down for the moment anyway and Saber hated sitting still for too long. She finished her paperwork, grabbed a satchel of clothes and things she would need and left with him. They didn't have women on their crew so Hank told her that she would stay in the Captain's quarters and he'd stay with the crew. She agreed it was fine and looked at the knife back at her belt, "Two swords feel better than a knife and a sword."

"Take a sword from our armory, just remember to return it when you are done," Hank shrugged, "I don't care."

Saber smiled with a wince at the stretching of her cheek, "Sweet."

The crew absolutely loved her, as was customary to them the crew trained as they traveled. Saber even injured was a force to be reckoned with and Hank chuckled when his first mate went head-to-head with her and it seemed a tie.

"Island!" their lookout called, "Dead ahead."

"Great," Hank sighed, "Too bad I hoped they were dead in the water."

They all stopped training and used the rest of the time to rest as much as possible. "If they aren't on the beach we will have to go searching for them. Landing crew plus Saber will be searching for them. Lucas is in charge. I'll stay at the ship with the rest of the crew in case they try to make a break for it."

It was an island the navy used to train on and Hank's crew was familiar with it, Saber told Lucas she had never been to the island before and he sighed, "I forget you went through training with the nobility. I don't hold that against you since you didn't have much say in it but it sucks."

"Thanks," Saber sighed, "The Old Man and Auntie always tried to keep me from any danger which was boring as hell."

Lucas laughed as they got on the landing boats. Saber helped the crew row in and when they landed Lucas said, "You are familiar with hunting right?"

"Yeah," Saber frowned.

"People?" Lucas pressed; he knew she was a fighter but not so much of her history. Saber stepped forward with the scouts and looked around, the sand gave them away. She pulled the swords and started walking, the crew hesitated as the scouts were still looking but they followed her after a quick look. Saber glanced back at the scout at her elbow, "You smell smoke?"

"Yeah, wind is heading toward the bay so it's from the valley."

"Their boat looks half repaired, why weren't they defending it?"

"Hard telling," he whispered back. She shrugged and they continued to walk. Saber held up a hand and the small twenty-man crew behind her froze and she laid on the ground to army crawl through the brush to see what was ahead. The scouts did the same, following her and cursing softly.

"They found the training camp and supplies," one whispered.

"Tell Lucas there are estimated at least fifty if not more. It's hard to count from this location since they are moving around," she looked at him, "I can watch them as we decide what to do about this."

They retreated back to the group and Saber laid there in silence. They were laughing and eating around a campfire. A pirate ran up and talked to Benji the Giant. He growled angrily, it seemed he was the captain of their ship. "We have the Marines on us, they are at the bay, get your weapons and prepare!"

His yell could be heard all over the clearing and Saber knew Lucas heard from behind her as well. They had followed their trail although the messenger came from the west so she wasn't sure where he had been before that. She slid carefully backward and crouched next to Lucas, "Messenger came from the west, not sure where he came from but that's how they know we are here."

"Let's get away from this trail before they head right for us," Lucas whispered back.

They moved quickly and quietly back down to a creek bed and followed it around a curve to avoid being seen from the trail they had followed. Saber unbuttoned her uniform jacket and spread mud over her pants quickly, her shirt was green—not standard issue but she always broke protocol because white was so hard to hide in. The mud and dirt was gross but she didn't care. She could wash in the creek after the fact. She glanced at the silent men studying her. She flashed a smile as she put mud on her face in a thin layer and stood going back around the bend. Lucas hissed after her demanding she get back there but she stayed in view of them, standing with her back to a tree, Saber stood motionless, only her eyes swiveled as she looked for any movement. The men noticed she blended into the scenery and they had a hard time seeing her even knowing she was there.

Pirates passed running fast, they could hear people running through the brush but when they were about to move she signaled with her hand to halt. They froze watching as she calmly stood in the open against the tree. Benji and four others walked behind their men talking about how to get out of this predicament. Saber waited until she couldn't see them, let alone hear them, before signaling they were good to move. Lucas came up to her with the small short-wave device to talk to Hank.

"I updated Captain, Saber," Lucas' voice stayed barely above a whisper as the men stayed hidden around the bend in case someone came back through. Lucas stood next to her but could easily hide behind the tree she leaned against.

"We plan to attack from the bay, stay clear of the beach, we won't aim any cannons toward the trees, if they want to protect their ship then they will need to reach us. They can't do that since we brought the boats back to the ship. Any thoughts?"

"Do you plan to completely take out their ship? Do we have enough man power to control this mob if we take them aboard?"

"Yes we do," Hank chuckled, "It will be a full house but it's doable although I understand your concern, they could overpower us."

"Two other ships are in the area," Lucas told her softly, being picked up by the transponder, "They can hear you as well."

"How close are they? It's one thing to blow up their ship but I don't like facing off with them being outnumbered two almost three to one."

"This is the Gable," another voice murmured into the transponder, "We are on the south side of the island. It will take us some time to get across to you but two hours is more than enough time."

"This is the Nutcracker, we are on the east side and over the hill from where the bay is. We could sweep up and over."

Saber looked to Lucas and noticed he was watching her expectantly, "What's that look for?"

"Everyone in Admiral Oliver's fleet knows you were raised in the borderlands and better at land fights than us seafolk," Lucas chuckled softly.

"I don't know the island, I've never been here before," she growled, "If anything I'd say if we blew up the ship they would scatter so holding off would make more sense to me. As for the east, I'd cover the uniforms in mud to camouflage yourselves and wait and watch, see if you can find them without losing the high ground. We wait for the Gable crew to get here. No one leaves boats on the shore and leave enough crew on the ships to maneuver them if need be. That gives us about even odds if we have 60 people total right?"

"Sounds perfect," Lucas grinned.

"Shut it, Benji the Giant is no joke. One swipe of his club nearly took a leg completely off in the last fight. If they have others like that then we might still be up a creek."

Things were underway and three hours later the pirate ship was reduced to smoldering ash while the three naval crews fought the pirates to capture them all. Benji proved to be more than Saber realized. Lucas tried to fight him and Saber went to assist when she saw Lucas was outmatched. That's the last thing she remembered.

Chapter 2

"Saber Aldara Barca for your bravery in battle, you are awarded a Naval Star of Excellence," Admiral Oliver announced to the crowd in the courtyard of the headquarters. The fight was weeks ago, Saber still had broken ribs and could barely stand although she stood still as Oliver pinned the star to her jacket. The crowd cheered but she didn't smile. Lucas and five others died. Benji was dead but that was little consolation.

"We will speak about your requests later, Saber," Oliver whispered for her ears only.

Saber got off the stage with a salute and frowned as Hank touched her shoulder, it was a memorial to honor those that passed as well as the three ships that went after the wanted criminal, Benji the Giant had a bounty of a million silver pieces, the generic merchant currency was by weight of silver or gold. As a Navy the bounty would be paid to the kingdom by all the other kingdoms that posted the bounty. The financial responsibility was by a family of merchants that deal in money. They guarantee delivery even to the most remote islands. They were partnered with lawyers the known world over and accompanied the lawyers in special circumstances. Saber stopped and ducked her head slightly as Hank's hand squeezed her shoulder.

"I'm sorry Captain, I tried to help but I...I don't even know what happened. It's all blank, I don't even remember the fight with Benji. This star should go to Lucas' family," Saber started to undo it but Hank caught her hand.

"They are getting a different star today, Saber. It's not your fault. You nearly died too, probably a blessing you don't remember the fight. You were so bloody and injured, we didn't think you would make it."

"I wish I was stronger," she whispered, "I'm not staying the rest of the ceremony, I'm going to slip out the back unless you need me."

"Oliver said you had a few requests and tried to refuse the honor, what were your requests?"

"Permission to train with both swords, I may not remember the fight but I know I would have died without both swords. Second was I wanted off the Admiral's ship, I...asked to join your crew although originally I asked to resign from the Navy. I want to journey further than the coast but feel I would be a burden on anyone as weak as I am now."

"You aren't weak, that's why you won that fight, Saber," he frowned, "I requested something quite similar. We cannot wait for all our members to heal as we have more and more merchants needing to travel. We do long range trips and need to leave in three days time. I asked for you to come with us since his ship was messed up and in the shipwright's care. Although I wouldn't mind stealing you out from under his first mate. I can't promise our crew could teach you as well as James could."

"To be honest he taught me a lot, it's just sheer strength that keeps me from beating him. I need more fights under my belt before I could beat him."

"Very true," Hank murmured, "If you are slipping out, go now while everyone is busy. The families will be at the reception hall and you need to be there for that, Saber. It's an order for all involved and you can't shirk your responsibilities."

"Yes sir," she slipped out the side door, and disappeared down the dark side hallway. Saber found stairs to a garden in the back of the HQ ballroom. She climbed up the railing and onto a pillar wincing at the throbbing pain in her side not to mention her arms and legs. She felt like an entire village took turns pummeling her. Saber sat on the pillar looking at the huge water fountain in the garden, folding her right leg under her left, the dress uniforms had white cloaks which hung down the side of the pillar although she didn't care about that. No one was there so she wasn't worried about it.

Two hours passed and she heard voices coming out of the doors, "I thought you said she came through the hall toward the garden, Hank?"

Admiral Oliver's voice was dulled, as though all emotion had been wrung from him. Hank agreed, "I watched her head out the back of the ceremony hall. The guards out front said she didn't go that way, she has to be here somewhere."

"That girl is like a cat, when you want to find her, she's nowhere to be found," Oliver rubbed his eyes, "Lucas' family wants to meet her."

"Is that wise?" Hank asked seriously.

"Yes, you might not know them well, Hank but they are good people. His parents and sister are aware she has amnesia of the fight," Oliver sighed, "Do you know what she has requested?"

Hank stayed quiet and Oliver sat on the top step staring at the fountain as he continued, "She asked to resign for not being strong enough. When that was denied she asked to be removed from my ship and to your own. I am not sure her reasoning but I am concerned for her mental health, Hank. I will let her go with you on this next trip of yours but we will readdress a permanent placement afterward. As for her training with dual swords, no one in the country has that training, however you will be going to the Zosha, right?"

"Yes sir," Hank agreed.

"We are on good terms with them," Oliver rubbed his chin, "Isn't that where Axel is from?"

"Yes but he isn't in the military there, he was trained from a young age but last time I crossed paths with him he was still too young to join the military and made no comments toward wanting that future."

"Maybe you can find him while you are there. By the time you get there, if all goes well she will be healed. Even one fight would teach her more than you would expect," Oliver murmured.

"To be honest our navy could benefit from training on land with the army. I know Saber wasn't taught by the army but the way she can track and camouflage herself was impressive to Lucas and his land crew. I just wish I had realized Benji the Giant was the same Giant Benji on that bounty, we would have revised the plan."

"Who came up with the plan anyway?"

"Although we knew the terrain, Saber came up with the plan. I wish more recruits were trained in tactics like that. Most the navy have to go to school after being at sea for a while, Saber had no idea of the terrain but after a brief map of the island from Lucas, she quickly came up with a plan and we all agreed to it. I don't know what happened but Saber was across the beach at one moment and appeared next to Lucas when he turned to face Benji. I don't know what made her move so fast, she was supposed to watch and assist where needed but the fight hadn't even started yet."

"Sixth sense maybe?" Oliver rubbed his head, "Has she asked about the fight and what happened? I've questioned her extensively and she doesn't remember anything no matter how hard we try."

"I watched...helplessly as I tried to get to the shore but she hasn't asked much. She feels responsible for Lucas' death although it wasn't her fault."

Oliver stood and dusted his breeches off as he turned to Hank, "It wasn't anyone's fault, things happen and you need to learn from it and make sure it doesn't happen again. That's all you can do. Moving on will take time. For a young lady who doesn't have the fruit or rare vegetable powers, she is powerful and worth her weight in gold. If she decided to eat any of that to acquire power, I would tell you to detour whether the merchants liked it or not."

"True," Hank nodded, "What's—hey Saber, why didn't you say something?"

Saber had laid back to stare at the sky. She looked over and sat up again, "Sir?"

"We were looking for you, why didn't you say anything?" Hank frowned.

"Permission to stay here the rest of the event, I'm still technically on the grounds, sir," she sighed.

"No, get down here."

She sighed and carefully turned to drop onto the landing at the top of the stairs. She winced grabbing her side as she slowly straightened, "Tell me the truth of the fight, every time I ask people they avoid it all together by saying it's a miracle I'm alive. What happened? I remember heading over to Lucas and Benji and that's it. If I have to meet his family, I want to know the story."

"Okay, Saber," Oliver sighed, "Hank will tell you everything that transpired."

"Alright," Hank sighed. She had fought with Lucas, both blocking Benji's swings which were powerful enough to fling one of them back. They had to work together to survive even a swing. Saber attacked fast between each attack, Lucas did the same, they were slowly working through it but Benji surprised Lucas with attacking with his fist. He was knocked to the ground, Saber continued to fight standing over his lifeless form. A few tried to move forward to help her but she yelled at them to stay back. She used the swords to deflect the swings as best as possible while also avoiding the random fisted attacks Benji hit her with. She couldn't move too far or he would target Lucas. Saber refused to let that happen so tried to fight as if someone had tied one hand behind her back.

She shocked them all with pulling a crazy move that sent Benji off balance and instantly threw all her weight into him, driving her swords into his chest and pressing the giant back so that he didn't fall on Lucas. She fell, a navy guy caught her quickly and laid her gently down. Benji was the last pirate down. Hank continued play by play, "You protected him, Saber, and even when you dropped you demanded of the officer who caught you to give you a sword."

Saber looked down, "How did Lucas die though?"

"That blow to the skull, it cracked it and killed him instantly. There was nothing you could do, Saber."

"What made you go to help him in the first place," Oliver asked, he had asked it before but wanted Hank to hear her.

"During the first fight he had barely swung that club of his and broke Will's leg. If he had been trying it would have removed the leg and two other people in the process. I could tell he was strong and we needed to avoid a direct blow but Lucas hadn't fought or seen the man before so I went to try helping him."

"You did good," Oliver met her gaze, "You heard what we were talking about before correct?"

"Yes sir," Saber nodded.

"Then come along, a certain old man and auntie are looking for you as well," Oliver smiled.

"Old man and auntie?" Hank cocked his head confused.

"Ulric and Giselle Thompson," Saber walked beside him as they followed the Admiral.

"You call General Thompson old man?" Hank stopped dead in his tracks.

"There is a story you are missing there," Oliver chuckled, "Ulric took her in when she was thirteen and caught picking pockets in the capital."

"You...you're the girl then," Hank stared at Saber who had paused to look at him confused.

"The girl?" she questioned, "I'm female but I have no idea what you are talking about, Captain Hank."

"Three and a half years ago there was an incident on our beach, we were in the harbor that day and were shocked to find pirates around under the guise of merchants. Giselle was here with a young girl and the girl protected her and ended up taking on three grown men at once."

"That was Saber's fourteenth birthday," Ulric appeared with his hands in his pockets.

"Hey Old Man don't go telling everyone my secrets," Saber snarled at him as Giselle stepped forward and hugged Saber gently touching bandages on her face and hands and talking quietly to her asking if she was alright.

Saber shot another glare back at Ulric as Giselle pulled her along. Ulric glared right back.

"Enough with the Old Man stuff, I am not old!" he growled.

Saber ignored him as she told Giselle she was fine and that it was just a few broken ribs but they would heal quickly and she felt fine. Ulric stepped toward her ignoring Oliver and Hank who were watching the three. He touched her hair and said, "I'll get gray hair if you make me worry you idiot girl."

Saber looked up at him about to make another snide comment but noticed his warm brown eyes tracking every bandage and bruise on the skin he could see. She met his gaze and smirked, "More training is on the horizon."

"Good," Ulric agreed, "Come on it's time to eat and celebrate the lives we lost."

Saber looked at Hank and Oliver, both were smiling amused and Ulric growled at them to quit making faces or he'd give them a reason to make a face. The Admiral walked next to Ulric who had Giselle on his arm, Hank and Saber brought up the rear.

Two days were quick and then she was on the ocean again. Two merchant ships in front of them leading the way to the islands. Because it was a long voyage Hank let his crew dress however they wanted as long as they had their weapons on hand. Knowing how Hank operated, Saber had clothes for the occasion. She wore cut off t-shirts and pants, she never wore shorts since her legs were riddled with scars. The crew were happy to have her aboard again. In the down time, Hank asked her for her story of how she came to find Ulric Thompson and live with him. It was just them near the helm which Mason was steering but he was a quiet guy and trustworthy from what she had learned from Lucas months before.

"The honest truth?" Saber asked sitting cross-legged on the deck.

Hank nodded, "I want to know how you know so much about hunting and tracking on land."

Saber wasn't in a story telling mood but as the captain of the ship she was obligated to tell him what he wanted to know. She turned her back to him and lifted her shirt, showing the large tattoo on her back of the RNB emblem. Hank stared at her as she lowered the shirt and walked away.

Mason glanced at him as Saber got out of earshot, "Do I need to teach our new crewmate manners sir? She showed the tattoo but I didn't recognize it."

"Don't mention it to anyone, Mas," Hank murmured softly, "That was the RNB mark. Bandits who were wiped out years ago. She must be a kid who survived the massacre."

"Does that answer your question though?"

"It does," Hank nodded, "Every kid raised in the RNB were trained since the time they could walk. No wonder she doesn't want people to pry too hard into her life. The Admiral knows since the incident three years ago, I'm sure Ulric explained how she could fight three grown men at fourteen."

"She's a monster when she fights," Mason agreed.

"I want her to stay with us," Hank admitted, "You think the crew would support that since she's a girl?"

"She can fight, I don't see why not. We need a bigger ship though sir, your snoring can wake the dead," Mason smirked as Hank growled that it wasn't funny. The crew did their tasks and Saber fell into the habit of a recruit new to a ship by doing the cleaning and helping with menial tasks although they had a recruit to do it. Hank told her to rest up, she needed to heal if she was going to meet Axel and the crew agreed. Everyone was still fresh from the last fight and had seen her face off the giant trying to protect Lucas.

Two long, for Saber they were impossibly long, weeks passed on the big blue ocean with nothing but water surrounding them before the doctor cleared her for activities. She came out of the doc's sick bay and stretched up feeling nearly perfect although sometimes she still had a pain or two she ignored that. Hank leaned over the railing to meet her gaze as she looked up at the sky. "Well, Saber?"

"Freedom never felt better, who's ready for exercise because I'm stir crazy!"

"Take it easy the first few days, Saber, you might be cleared but we don't want you pulling anything since you've been healing," Hank grinned, "Mason will dance with you."

"Wait what? I will?" Mason looked surprised as she moved to the center of the deck and turned to look at him. He was the helmsman but now had taken the first mate position as well since Lucas passed. He was also the strongest on the ship, although Saber had never fought Captain Hank to know if he was stronger than the captain as well. Mason wore a long sleeved shirt rolled to the elbows and unbuttoned with shorts, his six pack flexed as he jumped over the railing and landed on the deck across from her. She kept her swords sheathed as were the rules of training on the ship. Mason did as well although he pulled the knife from his belt, sheath and all. He attacked fast and hard, he was a thinker and Saber found him interesting when she fought him. He thought outside the box and kept her off balance as much as possible but her own planning seemed to jump and continue to move along without much stress for Saber since she was used to plans going out the window. Her mind just jumped to another sequence of moves. The entire crew watched in silence as they fought, she heard someone say three silver on her and Mason frowned, "What the hell, Andy there are no bets you idiot. You'll clean the ship with our recruit for that!"

Saber didn't laugh, she knew Mason could talk and fight at the same time and he was good at compartmentalizing. She turned quickly when she knew she wouldn't be able to guard against a surprise swipe, the sheath slammed against the deck as Saber swiped at him since he was open suddenly. Mason skipped back and they watched each other, it was a mind game it seemed with long pauses and equally long series of strikes. Hank chuckled as they methodically targeted each other's weak points and continued to fight long and hard. "Alright you two, that's it for today. We can't wear our newly healed Saber out, Mason."

"Of course not, Captain," Mason smirked, "You used to fall for some of those feints I'd throw in but I guess you know me too well now."

"You still surprise me though," Saber shook her head, "It's good to spar with you so I don't lose my edge. I like to think ten steps ahead but you like to pound a new cog in the wheel and see how it will run without warning."

Mason smirked at her analogy, "It didn't work though. You weren't going all out and I wasn't pushing either. It was a good exercise though."

"Yeah," she nodded.

They went up and sat on the stern deck which set above the men who were exercising next. They sat facing the railing, Saber stuck her legs between the rails to dangle down, to watch. "You showed Hank your tattoo. How did you make it that young from the border to the capital though?"

Saber hesitated, aware he didn't speak loud enough for anyone but Hank to hear them. She knew as the first mate he needed to understand her better so he could utilize her to the best ability. Secrets never stayed in the dark, she knew that but she had hoped this one would die. "I was raised in the woods, my father would dump us three miles outside the village and tell us to survive a week then come back to the village when we were growing up."

"We?" Mason asked quietly glancing at her.

"My older brothers and I," she nodded once.

"Where are they?"

"My entire family is dead," Saber's voice grew cold, "After this conversation I never want this brought up again, okay?"

"Sure," he nodded.

"The week of the massacre my father ordered all the kids to take off out of the village toward Ruld. Ex-communication, after announcing it to the village he told me that my brothers died scouting for the enemy and that he wasn't leaving. People had to stay behind to hold off the enemy. So I traveled for months, surviving in the woods since I had no money. I got to the capital and was caught picking pockets. The judge sentenced me to correctional school or whatever it was he called it. The Old Man and his wife took me in and taught me to read and write. Sad to say I knew how to fight before I knew how to cook, clean or even read and write. All I knew was war, even when you relaxed you always had an eye on your surroundings and listening to the woods around the village. If the birds stopped chirping or anything felt off."

"Who was the judge that took you in?"

"Old Man Thompson," Saber mumbled.

"What?" Mason jerked in shock and she frowned at him when a few of the crew glanced toward them, "Sorry, so...General Thompson took you in."

"Yeah," Saber nodded, "He liked to nag me to death about picking fights with bullies growing up. Once he figured out what was going on he started training me and even hired people to train me. Had I known that training to become a naval recruit would be so boring due to all that training I may have changed my mind."

"Boring?" Mason smirked surprised, "That is probably true since you were with the nobles, they always have an easier time of it."

"Mas," Hank said softly, "Our merchants are signaling, ask the crow's nest to report."

Mason took a deep breathe and yelled up to the nest for a report. They called back that they wanted to stop on an island to pick up supplies since they were running low being full of products to sell they didn't have as much food on the ship. Saber knew if the merchants had their way they would have stuffed the naval vessel with their products as well, seeing it as a sin for a ship to be empty as they travel. Hank told Mason to signal back an affirmative. They were two hours from an island and made it quick—food and gone since pirates were active in those waters and they didn't want any word of where they were heading leaked.

Mason glanced at Saber who was watching the fight below but almost as if her mind was somewhere else. "Saber did you eat any of the fruit or vegetables on the island when we went to training island?"

Saber shook her head, "No. Is it only found there?"

"They are extremely rare so when you find a patch it's guarded by military or government authorities although with you, I doubt you want powers right?"

"Does anyone here have power?"

"Yeah a few, although some of us didn't go through training at all," Mason snickered.

"How do you mean?"

"We were rehabilitated by Hank," Mason smirked, "I grew up on a pirate ship, a lot of us did actually. Hank's crew took out our ships and made sure we were raised in the port city if we weren't old enough to join the navy. Once we were old enough the Admiral had us tested on our knowledge of ships to the point that we didn't need training."

"I see," Saber looked back down at the training, the new recruit stepped up and asked one of the officers to spar, Hank let his crew ask for a particular partner. If they wanted to change their positions there was an official match when they docked somewhere—just like a pirate ship. The recruit was a year older than Saber and only ever asked one officer to spar, "Why does Lincoln only ever spar with Bradley?"

"Bradley I think is Linc's goal. That and because he's still young and didn't grow up on ships the crew is kind of rough on him."

"They aren't that way to me," Saber cocked her head meeting Mason's eyes confused.

"You haven't been part of the crew but there are many reasons for that," Mason looked down to watch the training. Saber had watched him progressively get better but he was still off balanced when he fought.

"What are the reasons?" Saber asked as Mason stood up and lit a cigarette as he moved to the side of the ship to toss his match.

"First off you are a lady and I don't stand for mistreating women," Hank started to answer her question.

"Second, you might be different but bandits are the equivalent of land pirates, you understand us better than most navy recruits would," Mason said.

"Is that all?" Saber shook her head still not understanding why the kid would be targeted.

"Most recruits come from families who served, they feel entitled or they grew up seeing the navy and wanted to join with no experience in fighting or at life in general. Most recruits stay recruits for five years before they are actually given a rank because they know nothing. You were in for less than six months and already jumped three ranks."

"Hm," Saber frowned seeing Lincoln get tossed off his feet and Bradley move back to what he was doing before getting asked to spar. Saber had noticed how Lincoln held his sword, "It'd help if someone taught the kid how to hold his sword right to start with."

"He's older than you, Saber," Hank chuckled.

"Well I'm cleared for cleaning duties again," Saber stood and moved toward Lincoln without a backward glance. Mason and Hank stared in surprise, she was part of the fighting crew so she didn't have to do anything with the sailing crew although she had been trained by all of them in case there was need for it.

"You shouldn't help with this," Lincoln told her frowning, "You aren't a recruit any more, Barca."

"I'm bored so let me help," Saber helped him clean and prep food. As they finished and lunch was being served, she asked, "Who taught you to fight?"

"Boot camp," he frowned, "Why?"

"Find me later," she stretched as she took her food and slipped out to Hank.

Hank frowned seeing two bowls in her hands but accepted the meal watching as the crew went in shifts to eat. Lincoln appeared soon after.

"Why did you ask that question?" he frowned meaning why she asked who trained him with the sword.

"Because you hold it like it is a stranger," Saber finished her food and set the bowl down studying him, "Spend time practicing the sequences they taught you and holding your sword, get used to every aspect of it. Also when you fight don't over extend, Bradley exposes your weaknesses and you are making a lot of progress working on them but a sword is sharp, right? So it's safe to assume an inch of blade will hurt just as much as a foot of blade, yes?"

Lincoln stared at her for a moment in surprise, "But training is with the sheaths so the stronger individual wins out."

"Not true," Mason appeared surprised Hank was eating already and steering with one hand, "Saber is smaller than me and I'm stronger than her but her strengths aren't muscle they are technique. I don't always win when I spar with her because she knows her way around a sword and plans her attacks. Don't get stuck on plans though because once you make them they go straight out the window, it's just to give you a starting point."

"It doesn't matter if you have a sheath, the point of training is to learn to anticipate any opponent not just the one in front of you. So practice what

I've said because I plan on sparing with you," Saber met his gaze as she sat on the deck looking up at him.

Lincoln nodded and took her bowl and the captain's to the dish room. Saber noticed the island was closer and asked Hank, "You planning on keeping us on the ship or are we getting off for a visit?"

"I forgot you asked to join us to explore islands didn't you," he chuckled, "Cook wants to replace what little food we have went through so you are volunteering to help him pack food along with Lincoln and a few others."

"Fun," Saber smiled standing to her feet.

"You really plan to help Lincoln fight better?" Mason asked her curiously.

"If he's willing to learn, I'm willing to teach, I know if I don't what the end result will be one day and I would rather avoid it. I'm not perfect but I can teach what I know if anyone wants a bout most can learn from sparring anyway. I won't refuse a challenger, I like to exercise and it only makes me better," Saber shrugged.

Life had a lot of fighting but there were things in life worth fighting for, Saber had come to realize, now she wanted to find out what those things were. She had both her swords on her hip and braided her hair out of her way as they slowed to the harbor. Eldridge, the cook, came up and Hank made quick orders for him to take Saber and three others with him. She walked with them and as they shopped she reached down to pick up a berry frowning at it, "What is this?"

"Good eye, it is a rare fruit of our island," a man smiled and Eldridge asked him what it was called.

"A silver for a piece of fruit?" Saber asked confused but if it was a rare fruit only found on their island then she wanted to try it and it explained why it was so much. She tossed it into her mouth as she grabbed a silver. Eldridge looked shocked that she just ate it as the merchant pointed out a vegetable that was also only found on their island. She paid for it too and ate both standing there, she looked at the crew to see them staring as if she lost her mind. "What? I wanted to say I ate something I'd never find at home. Is that so wrong?"

"Don't eat any more," Eldridge told her seriously, "Let's get our food and leave. Lincoln make sure she doesn't lose her mind or do anything else."

"Sir," Lincoln studied her with worry in his eyes.

"What am I missing," she frowned at them.

"Most the time you would have to pay gold for those types of fruits and vegetables, or go to the training island, Saber," Eldridge met her gaze seeing her face pale fast.

"You mean those were the power giving kind?" she whispered shocked.

"Yes and when you eat them they have different affects. We need to hurry, you ate two different kinds so who knows what will happen."

Saber was quiet as they hurried through the market. They got back to the ship and Hank looked surprised, "Get a good price?"

"I need to talk to you and the doc," Eldridge announced making everyone tense.

"What's wrong?" Hank frowned instantly.

"Saber ate a fruit and vegetable that can give powers...back to back," Eldridge announced and the crew nearly exploded in noise. Saber frowned around at all their worried faces.

"Calm down, I feel fine!" she growled at them.

"Saber remove your weapons and give them to Mason. You are confined to your quarters until doc clears you for duty, damn it why didn't you stop her, Eld?" Hank growled.

"It didn't register that she hadn't had the stuff before until she popped it into her mouth. She ate it before paying for them!"

Saber tensed, "Why can't I keep my weapons?"

"Because some hallucinate and attack anyone and anything in sight," Hank told her.

"I'll keep them close and as soon as you are cleared you can have them back, Saber," Mason stepped toward her. She looked to the doc and he said no more than six hours max.

Saber released her weapons and went to her room as the men stowed the food and they set sail soon after. The other ships were quick since they were nervous in a foreign port and pirates popular in the area. The doc came in every half an hour finding Saber exercising or reading a book each time. She did balancing exercises and arm exercises by doing one handed handstands and pushups. She read about the fish in the ocean and what was edible since she didn't know much about the ocean. He studied her and frowned, "How do you feel?"

"Like I want my weapons back because this is uncomfortable and I'm bored in here," she mumbled still reading.

"No weird feelings or anything?" he pressed.

"Nope," she sighed.

"Supper is nearly done. I'd like for you to stay without weapons until morning to be safe. No one has ever eaten two different things before so we are in unknown territory."

"Seriously, you said six hours max," Saber complained.

"That was before I realized it wasn't two different fruit but a vegetable and fruit," he growled.

"Fine," she sighed.

Late that night she had a high fever, Hank and Mason were informed, the entire crew was quiet. The group that went to shore were upset they hadn't stopped her but being from the woods they figured she had been aware of the dangers of those fruits and vegetables at least. Saber cried out names, the crew could hear her through the night yelling for people they didn't know and one that they did—Lucas. They knew she was having hallucinations but they didn't sound like anything good. When morning came the doctor looked exhausted but Saber was finally sleeping peacefully. Nearly lunchtime, Saber came out with her hair down and a tank top on. She met Mason's eyes as she stopped in front of him, "Weapons, sir."

"Doc?" Mason asked having three swords on his waistband since he promised to hold onto them for her.

"She's cleared," the doc informed them. Mason handed them over and could see her shoulders relax as she put the swords in her waistband.

"How do you feel, Saber?" Mason asked her directly.

"Like I will question any fruits or vegetables for the rest of my life," Saber tied her hair up into a ponytail instead of a bun or braid as she had before. She didn't say more as she moved to her place she liked to sit on the deck with her feet in-between the railing.

"It usually takes a few days to realize your power," Mason told her, "Did the merchant say anything about the type of fruit and vegetable you tried?"

"No," Saber didn't turn to look at him but watched the crew move around. They trained and Lincoln surprised her with asking her to spar with him. Bradley looked surprised having been setting down the fishing pole he was using. He turned to look up at her and one of the other men commented that he only had the balls to ask her because she was weak from the night of fevers.

Saber stood and said, "Whoever just said that, I want you next."

Everyone tensed at her tone as she came down the stairs. Lincoln met her gaze without a word. Saber pulled just one sword, sheathed, from her waist and fought with him. Saber barely blocked or just avoided his attacks. He caught his balance a few times and slowly started to adjust his stance to stay balanced as she fought with him. She angled the sword to glance off and ended the fight with the sword to his neck. "Keep practicing and remember what I said, Linc."

"Yes ma'am," he nodded as she turned and met the other man's eyes.

"Come," she didn't give him a choice. He pulled both a sword and knife. Saber looked at Lincoln, "Let me borrow your knife."

"Why not just use the two swords?" Lincoln frowned.

"I don't want to break him too badly," Saber didn't crack a smile. The knife was in her dominant hand, Hank realized as she attacked fast and hard. She was like a cyclone and the man could barely track her moves. She had touched him a total of twenty-three times in a matter of moments when she stood with the sword sheathed to his neck.

"Do I seem weak to you?" she asked him directly.

"No ma'am," he shook his head letting his sheathed weapons drop to the deck.

"Anyone who wants to learn or just wants to spar with me has an open invitation, if you think it's because I'm a girl that it's weak to spar with me, I will prove you wrong every time."

Saber tossed Lincoln the knife back and set her sword in her belt again before going back onto the stern deck to sit, this time she faced away from the lower deck and looked at the sky. Hank and Mason were grinning as they stood at the helm. Saber didn't ask what they were smiling about, she enjoyed the thuds of others sparing below and idle talking as the wind blew, pushing the ships on their journey.

It would take them three months more to get to the destination of Zosha Kingdom, the port city called Zosha was the capital. Two days after her hallucinations, Saber was still sleeping badly and dreaming of her siblings although she never cried out as she had during her fever. Mason wondered who those names belonged to for her, Saber surprised him when he joined her to watch men sparing on the stern deck, "Don't bring up the past, we agreed."

"I didn't ask anything, Saber," Mason frowned.

"You want to know the names I called out when I had the fever dreams," Saber shook her head.

"Yes but how did you know?" Mason asked glancing at Hank who was looking at Saber curiously too.

"I don't know, I just do," Saber shook her head.

"You seem tired, are you still dreaming about those people...and Lucas?" Mason asked ignoring her demand to not bring it up.

"It doesn't matter," Saber shook her head.

"Who are they?" Mason asked.

Saber glared at him, hard, but he studied her calmly as if it didn't bother him to wait for her to respond to her first mate. She looked at Hank to find him studying them as well and he nodded slightly. She looked back down at the sparing crew and sighed, "Pushy looks terrible on you, first mate."

"Doesn't matter," Mason shrugged.

"My village was massacred, most the names you probably heard were people I couldn't save...my father, my brothers, my friends and extended family. To be honest the only one I can hope to be alive is Ace, a brother I wouldn't even know if I passed on the street since he was taken before I was born to Lidsing."

"Wonder where Doc is," Mason frowned, "He might be able to give you a tea to make you quit dreaming."

"He's in the mess and I don't need any tea," Saber glared at him. Mason frowned but didn't say anything. Hank however knew that Saber hadn't seen or spoken to the doc all day, nor had she been below decks since lunch, so how did she know where doc was.

"Saber how do you know where doc is?"

"I don't know."

"Close your eyes," Hank murmured and she sighed feeling him wanting to test her.

"This isn't going to work, Captain, making me identify people around the ship."

"Where is Eldridge?" Hank didn't care what she said, he wanted to test it and also noticed that she practically read his mind. Hank and Mason watched as she pointed out all of them without fail. Even those that had disappeared from deck. Saber could tell Lincoln was hidden away in the ship practicing what she had told him.

Months passed, they went on the islands but Saber steered clear of any rare food, wanting to avoid any more headaches although they wouldn't bother her anymore since she developed powers that were similar in nature. The crew had turned shy knowing she could hear certain thoughts, worried she would hear thoughts not meant for a young woman's ears...or in this case mind thoughts. Saber grew up knowing men could have gutter trash for brains so wasn't worried about that, however she didn't always hear their thoughts, it was only if they were aimed at her or as if wishful thinking toward someone else not just thoughts to oneself.

Mason and Hank sparred with Saber although she also targeted some people and even summoned Lincoln a few times, giving more advise. Everyone she summoned, the rest of the crew could tell a difference in their fighting style.

Land was sighted as they finally made it to their destination. Saber studied the long dark line on the horizon, it looked like someone drew dark ink across the horizon but it was a lot longer than she expected since it was a continent not an island. Saber was excited to see what happened from here since there were Army guards in the marketplace for their kingdom's merchants to be protected upon arrival. Luckily Captain Hank told them that they didn't have to dress up in their navy uniforms when they landed since they would have shore leave for a while at least.

When they docked, Saber was surprised that Hank and Mason caught her arms, "Wait, we have someone to meet."

Saber frowned confused as Mason led them off the ship. Saber walked through the market and was surprised that everyone spoke the common tongue, Giselle had taught her more than just Ruld and Lid during her stay with the Thompson family. Saber could speak four languages, common and Zo being the other two. Zoshans spoke Zo and as the biggest importer into Ruld, Giselle taught Saber how to speak the language and even had her go to the market in every port city to pick up the accents and practice with Giselle.

"Commander, how are you?" a Ruld army officer asked as they neared the end of the dock.

"Good," Hank smirked. Mason noticed the confusion on Saber's face and leaned into her ear, "Army and Navy have different ranking systems but in the army the rank of Captain is the same as commander to them so to make life easier they just use their rank for him. They protect any visiting delegation visiting here and the Ruld Merchants while here."

Saber nodded slightly and heard Hank asking for Axel, if the officer knew where the kid would be found. "I don't know why you care about that ruffian but he's been hanging around the south end of the docks where the pirates and thugs hang out."

"Thanks," Hank looked up at Bradley who was watching the ship for a few hours, "Take care of her, we'll be back in a few hours for you to have some shore leave yourself!"

"Aye, Cap'n," Bradley gave a half salute and Hank led them to the south. They were dressed as if they were civilians. Kids ran wild around the docks and twice Saber reached down to swat a hand heading toward her captain and first mate's belt purses without notice. She didn't carry money on her belt, she kept hers tucked inside her breeches or in her breastband to keep from anyone getting to it. The kids looked shocked she caught them and when she let them go with a wag of her finger they scampered off surprised she wasn't screaming for guards.

The power she had received was just as loud as the fish market they passed through but she could tune it out, only noticing if it was aimed toward her group, it took a few islands along the way to get used to the noise in her head but Saber was a quick study. Hank had been irritated because he knew some took months or even a year to get used to their powers, knowing that Saber quickly adjusted he had calmed down and quit taking it out on the group that took her to the first market they found.

As they walked, Saber noticed it was definitely a rougher crowd. Mason glanced back once to check on her but said nothing, as if he were looking back to see if they passed their destination or not. Saber studied the docks, it reminded her of the market near RNB village. She couldn't help but feel a smile tug at her lips feeling at home.

"Hey lovely, come to the bar with me," a man called falling into step with Saber.

"Sorry handsome, I don't drink," Saber shook her head continuing to walk. Mason glanced back and studied the man with an amused smile.

"Not really your type either, right Barca?" Mason asked in Ruld.

"Not at all but I can't be rude," she said and looked back at the pirate switching to common, "Maybe later, I'm heading to a meeting with my captain and I don't think he'd wait."

Hank didn't stop or turn as he continued to walk. Saber didn't break her stride as the pirate looked surprised as she smiled moving on as he fell behind her. She didn't look like a pirate, who was she? He wondered. Saber ignored his thoughts as she walked.

They came to a large open area where bets were being placed against two pirates fighting. Hank sat watching without comment, Saber and Mason sat next to him as well watching. Hank touched Saber's arm, "Who do you think will win?"

"The red shirt," Saber didn't hesitate, she could tell he was holding back.

Mason chuckled, "I agree, cap."

They didn't notice looks their way, Saber felt eyes on her but didn't say a word more than asked as she watched the fight. Soon enough the red shirt won and flashed a smile when he looked around and his eyes fell on Hank who smirked.

He came up ignoring the celebrating pirates who bet on him, Hank stood and shook his hand, "Long time kid."

"What's up Hank?" he smiled, "It's been forever. Where's Lucas?"

"Dead," Hank shook his head. His eyes rounded in surprise; the gray color caught her interest, she had never seen eyes that color or ebony hair. No one in Ruld had hair and eyes like that. Saber herself had blue eyes but her hair was strawberry blond. Most Ruld had blue or green eyes, rarely brown.

"Sorry, I didn't know."

"Axel I'd like you to meet Saber Barca and Mason Logans," Hank introduced them, "Mason usually stays on the ship when we visit you. Saber is a new recruit, Admiral Oliver said to ask you to train her for the few months we are here."

"I don't train people," Axel shook his head.

"Would you like to see her fight?" Hank asked seriously, "If anything fight her yourself."

"Anyone willing to try their hand against our strongest fighter here today?" the announcer said. Saber looked down to see a fighter with one sword. She pulled one sword off and handed it to Mason and stood. She tied her hair up out of her way and raised her hand as she headed to the stairs. The announcer froze watching her.

"You don't have to do this, he will kill you," Axel started to catch her arm but she yanked out of his grip and glared at him. He froze, her eyes had a way of chilling people to the bone when she was ticked off. She didn't do it because Hank offered, she did it because she hadn't fought hard in days and she was seriously bored.

She tightened her ponytail and came onto stage easily, the announcer frowned, "Your name?"

"Saber."

"Seriously what's your name?"

"Saber Barca," she met his gaze.

"I noticed you had two swords, girl," her opponent started, "Go ahead and fight with both, my sword technically is two in one."

Saber cocked her head and he did something to his sword and it split the sword into two. She turned and nodded to Mason who chucked her sword toward her. She slid it into her waistband and pulled both swords. Saber turned back to face the man she was going to fight and nodded, "Teach me something good, got it?"

"Teach? You'll be lucky to keep your head, girl," he smirked.

"We'll see," she shrugged and heard his thoughts, *It's your head and I hope you are ready for the instant attack because I attack right at the signal.*

Saber held her swords as if an extension of her arms, the signal started and she blocked the surprise attack with ease. She attacked fast and hard, he kept up with her and grinned surprised. They continued to fight and she avoided all the dangerous attacks most fell for. She skipped backward to avoid a swipe to her throat and found herself at the very edge of the ring which was three foot up from the beach. He swiped again and she jumped down to avoid the attack completely. The man grinned as she put her swords up, they had been fighting for almost half an hour. He put his sword up and offered her a hand up but she waved him off, "You won this round, I'm going back to my seat."

"Very well, girl," he murmured, "Tell me one thing before you go."

"What's that?" she looked up at him as she untied her hair again.

"Where the hell are you from?"

"Here and there, I traveled a lot growing up," she shrugged, "I was born in Ruld. Why?"

"You fight differently than many around here," he smiled.

"Thanks for the compliment I guess," she smirked and walked away, shocked they applauded her as she walked. She glanced at Hank and Mason seeing two kids sitting with them, they were the two that Saber had stopped from stealing from Mason and Hank. She ignored them as she sat behind Hank and Mason quietly. The two kids looked shocked at Saber, completely floored that she actually could fight and was easy going.

"So your name is Saber Barca?" Axel asked.

"That's me," she said watching the next match.

"Fine, I will give you some pointers," Axel met her gaze.

"When and where?" Hank asked. If you wanted to make sure it didn't look like you were discussing business, talk while watching other things without turning to look at the person. Saber had learned that growing up, she didn't make eye contact at all with Axel, she slouched on the bleacher style seats and when someone complained she was taking too much room, her unwavering gaze made them back down.

"Tomorrow, your ship," Axel murmured, "I take it that hasn't changed?"

"Nope," Hank murmured, "We are docked north of the fish market and just south of the fabric vendors."

"See you at dawn then," Axel glanced up in surprise that the three stood instantly and walked away. Saber stretched as she let Mason and Hank pass her.

"What's wrong Saber?" Mason asked.

"Now can I explore or are you going to ball and chain me back to the ship?"

"After the stunt you pulled I refuse to let you start trouble being alone," Hank shook his head, "Someone needs to make sure you don't get into trouble you heathen."

"Captain, I'm an angel, don't you see my halo?" Saber complained as she took the first step.

"A halo who uses those stickers before discussing issues and tries things without thinking first," Mason chuckled glancing back at her.

"It's not my fault I was sheltered as a kid," she said sarcastically.

"Right," Hank sighed, "Come on."

Saber continued to stop pick pockets without throwing a fuss about catching them. They were orphans on the ship docks trying to survive. Mason caught her leaning forward to swat another hand and missed the culprit who was in his blind spot, "Problems?"

"Next time we go for a walk, make sure you secure your belongings better," she grumbled at him.

Mason flashed an amused smirk and she realized they did it to test her. Saber didn't say anything more about it, she went to the ship with them and when Bradley started to leave she asked him where he was heading. He glanced at her and to Hank for a moment.

"Not somewhere you would want to visit," Bradley didn't say more and she didn't need to know.

"Captain please just turn me loose, I won't eat anything and I won't leave the docks," she crossed her heart and he smirked, "Fine."

She jerked her fist in the air and skipped back down the plank to the dock. She knew Bradley had been there before and asked where she could find a book vendor. He pointed toward the south again and she thanked him before shoving her hands in her pockets as she walked. She walked for a while, moving off the beach front and further into the market, finding animals she had never seen before. She paused to look at some and a younger girl sat at the vendor booth with an old man the girl asked hesitantly in Zo, "Looking to buy?"

"Just looking, I've never seen animals like these before," Saber shook her head speaking Zo which surprised the old man who could tell she was foreign, "What do you call them?"

She got a lesson on the local animals and what they were used for, some were just exotic and sold for pets to people outside the kingdom. The old man chuckled as the little girl explained everything and didn't complain that Saber needed to move along. Saber asked questions and the little girl really knew her stuff. Saber smiled and handed over a silver piece, "Thanks for the information. You really know your stuff so keep up the good work."

"Thanks!" the little girl tucked the silver away in surprise, hiding it from the old man who wasn't fooled.

Saber moved on and found books soon after and found a lot of books she really wanted. She bought six books and accepted them wrapped in paper. She turned and found the man she had sparred with staring at her. "You are still roaming around? It's nearly dark, you don't want to be out around here without someone to watch your back."

"I didn't realize it was that late," Saber glanced up at the sky.

"I'll walk with you," he frowned.

"Dom," Axel appeared from an alleyway, "What are you doing here?"

"I found a stray," the tall man told him with an easy smile of amusement.

"Saber right?" Axel asked looking at her.

Saber didn't say anything just turned to head back to the docks, Axel stopped her, "What are you still doing out here without a leash anyway?"

"Shore leave what else?" Saber frowned, "It's not against the law to shop is it?"

"No," Axel scoffed and switched from Common to Zo, "She giving you trouble?"

"Nah, I told her I'd walk her to the ship since it's getting late and these streets can be rough," Dom responded.

"I can take care of myself, thanks all the same," she met Axel's eyes with a glare speaking Zo as well.

"Yeah and Hank will kill me if anything happens to you, princess," he smirked, surprised she knew the language, "So let us escort you back."

"Do what you want, I'm leaving," she brushed his hand off her arm and moved toward the docks. She found Mason closer to the ship and he was with Eldridge and a few other crew members who were drunk and swaying their way back toward the ship. She glanced at Dom and Axel, "See you around."

She melded into the group and Dom and Axel watched them walk off hearing one man, Eldridge, call, "Saber! You were let loose on this poor town?"

"You're drunk, Eld, let's get you Neanderthals back to the ship before they think you were let loose on the poor town," Saber retorted.

"You find what you were looking for?" Mason asked her.

"No but I found some books and a very nice kid explained the wildlife around here which was fun. Maybe tomorrow," Saber told him.

"Come on, Saber, what are you looking for?" Lincoln asked her.

"I'll know it when I find it, are you all blasted drunk?"

"Not drunk," Lincoln was flushed.

"Mason told Linc that he needed to let loose, so Linc is drunk," Eldridge laughed.

"You are a bunch of foolish men," she sighed with a laugh, "I'm not a leaning post for you, Mason, get off."

"I'm not leaning," Mason argued although he was definitely leaning.

"I'm hungry," Eldridge complained.

"Then you can cook for us on the ship," Mason laughed, "I'm hungry too!"

"I don't want to cook," Eldridge groaned.

"If you don't mind, I'm craving something and I will cook if I can borrow your kitchen, Eld," Saber asked.

"Sure," Eld nodded, "Make it good though."

She paused glancing around and walked across to a vendor who looked nervous since he was about to shut down for the night and seeing a bunch of men who looked like pirates walking by wasn't sure if they were going to ruin his booth or rob him blind. Saber asked for seven things and once she had it she paid him extra since she knew he was about to close up. She corralled them back to the ship ignoring or not noticing Axel shadowing them with his friends.

Saber cooked quickly and brought it out to the group sitting on deck waiting. She ate a bowl and sighed, the mental pressure from town had eased since most had already went to bed. Mason groaned, "What is this stuff?"

"That is uh...well it's called Bandit's Delight," she didn't lie about the name since that's what bandits called it and it was a unique RNB recipe her family held.

"Bandit's Delight huh?" Eldridge studied her, "It's delicious. Give me the recipe."

"Not going to happen," she flashed a smile, "Those who know the recipe will die before giving it up."

"I'll just have to make it myself and see if I can replicate it," Eld grinned liking the challenge.

"You can try but there is a special ingredient that you won't find," Saber smirked.

"And what's that?"

"You have to be a bandit at heart," she laughed surprising them. Hank tried a bowl and stared at Saber in surprise, "Here I thought you couldn't cook to save your life."

"Don't ask me about fish but if you need someone to hunt and cook, I'm all about it," Saber shrugged, "I can cook anything from the woods."

Hank nodded and noticed her package of books, "More books I see. I guess Giselle really gave you a desire for books huh?"

"She taught me to read and write," Saber shrugged and stood, "Good night guys, I'm going to read for a bit."

"Don't forget dawn you have a visitor," Mason told her.

"I know," Saber walked away.

Hank and Mason were concerned that Axel was hanging with the pirate crowd but decided to let Saber continue with Admiral Oliver's plan. Saber woke the next morning and found Dom and Axel both on the ship talking to Hank for a moment. She stretched as she walked and turned when Eldridge called her name. She was still stretching up and caught the roll he tossed to her. Dom and Axel both noticed the tattoo but didn't recognize the design since she was pretty far away. Most with tattoos located on the back stood for having a history of trouble with the law. She was too young to be that bad at least they thought so wondered about her story. She came toward them and Axel lifted his chin slightly. Dom stood and asked her to pull her swords.

Saber pulled her swords and Dom instructed her for a long time, it was nearly noon when they finished. The entire crew had watched from around the deck as Saber dripped sweat without saying a word. Dom glanced to Axel who nodded slightly and they stood to leave. Saber sheathed her swords and turned toward her room. She took a long shower and then found Hank and Mason on deck waiting with food for her. She ate with them and they told her that four were stationed on the ship and the rest had shore leave. Saber could continue to explore. She hesitated and looked at Hank, "They haven't asked why we requested training have they?"

Hank wouldn't tell her that they got the story of Lucas' death and how she had fought Benji the Giant. They asked her story but Hank had refused to say, although they pressed the issue plenty. "We haven't said a word about your history. They don't know about you and they don't like it. Watch your back if you go to the market again."

"Don't worry, I will be an upstanding citizen," Saber smiled moving to shore and wanting to find a journal so she could write about some of the things she found. She couldn't draw for crap but she wanted to write down what she learned. As she headed back where she had stopped the night before a fight broke out at a bar and Robert, the sail hand on her crew, was surrounded. Saber sighed seeing the group was eight to one. She stepped into the middle of their loose circle and looked to Robert, "What'd you do this time?"

"Evidently a bar maid is taken and I was a little too forward," Robert watched them.

"Let us through," Saber told the one guy, he smirked and declined.

"Newbies need to learn their lesson," the guy in front of the bar said looking like a piece of work.

"You know girls don't have signs over their heads saying they are taken, maybe you should remember that and warn a guy before he gets his hopes up," Saber told him.

"Who are you, his mommy?"

"No, his ma is back home knitting us sweaters for when we get back," Saber pulled her swords and sighed, "Cap'n will have my head since I promised not to raze the town."

"I'll take the punishment," Robert told her. She surprised the pirates in front of her, taking the head honcho who talked big first. He was a good fighter but she used the blunt of her blade to knock him out. Those watching the fight thought it was a dance, Robert had another tough opponent so Saber took two on the left that seemed to realize the guy who wanted to fight was down and they should do something, the rest stepped back wanting to run but their pride was on the line. A call of guards coming was heard and they all put their swords up and hurried to walk away. Only those on the ground were seen as fighting. Saber glanced at Robert to see a cut on his cheek, she met his gaze, "Ask a girl if she's taken. Most bar maids flirt for more tips so if someone gets upset it should be at her for being too forward with patrons but men can't think logically it seems. You good from here?"

"Yeah, I'm heading back to the ship for duty anyway."

"Later," Saber moved on stretching up again, unaware that her tattoo was visible again and that she had shadows hounding her steps. She got to the book vendor and found a journal. She looked at weapons as well and asked questions of the vendor but decided against buying anything. She had money saved from the months on the Admiral's ship but she had to use company issued weapons which were better made than those the vendor was selling. She heard gambling on down and started to head that way although the vendor warned her not to. She stayed back far enough not to be seen, it was under the bleacher seats they had been at the day before. She stepped up on the scaffolding of the bleachers and looked over everyone's heads to see that in the heat of the day they were fighting under the bleachers out of the sun. She didn't move as two appeared at her sides, "We'd like a word, Ms. Barca."

"Who sent you?" she didn't look at them. Their thoughts were worried she would try to fight them since they were ordered not to touch a hair on her head, just escort her to Axel and Dom and Saber could hear them.

"Dom," the other responded. She nodded and followed them away from the fight and into the shade across the street and into a building. She found ten men sitting around the warehouse room, Axel and Dom sitting facing her.

"To what do I owe this pleasure?" Saber asked not reaching for her weapons.

"We have a question your Captain and First Mate refuse to answer. They said your past is for you to tell and to ask you but it seemed that your crew doesn't know your story."

"You know Captain Hank well, yes?" Saber met his gaze calmly.

"Yes but suddenly Lucas is gone and you appear. I want to know your story of how you came to be with them and where you came from. That mark on your back gave us a hint something was off."

"And if you don't like my story?" Saber asked.

"You may disappear," Axel was curious to what she would do with the threat but she shrugged.

"I was born in RNB village on the border between Ruld and Lidsing. RNB stands for Ruld North Bandits, their history is long and they weren't always considered bandits but that's a story for another day."

"RNB," Axel's eyes narrowed.

"A lot happened growing up but ultimately I landed in the Navy. Technically I am assigned a different ship but Captain Hank requested me to join his crew for this trip because he was down seven fighting men."

"Tell us the full story, wench," another man growled, "If you were a bandit how the hell did you get into the Navy?"

Saber wouldn't see these men after they left...and even if she did it wouldn't harm her to tell the truth, it was easier than fighting them all. She sighed mentally shrugging, "When I was 7 years old I received my mark, tradition dictates that a mark is given when a life is taken. I didn't want the mark, I hated all the fighting however when you are born into RNB you fight or you die. At 13 the entire village was massacred by Lidsing, just before it fell the children and teenagers were ex-communicated and told to disappear, forcing us to leave but not knowing how many survived. I traveled alone for a bit and landed in hot water picking pockets in the capital. The judge ruled I needed discipline and took me in. I grew up traveling with the judge and his wife."

"How'd you join the Navy?" Axel watched her, he was surprised she was telling the truth although he was well aware it was an abridged version.

"I want to see the world so Judge Thompson trained me and sent me to the boot camp. I was assigned to the Admiral's ship when pirates appeared. One pirate ship out of six got away. Captain Hank although his crew travels away from the Ruld kingdom our ship's crew are close to them so I knew him from many collaborations near the coast. Captain Hank was asked to go after the ship and because I saw the direction and fought against them, I was sent with them to give information about the crew I had noticed. Benji the Giant was on that ship although I had no idea who that was. The pirate ship landed on Boot Camp Island, Ruld's training outpost for navy recruits. L—Lucas was leading the landing party and because I grew up as a bandit I knew more about tracking and locating people so Captain Hank sent me along. Most Captains assigned to HQ know about my history in case I land on their ships. Anyway, sixty pirates against 20 navy wasn't going to work so other ships in the area came to assist. When we launched a surprise attack to capture the pirates they were fighting for their lives and Lucas was facing off with Benji. I had seen Benji barely swing his club and nearly take a man's leg off so I went to assist him. I don't remember the fight, a glancing blow to the head or something caused it. Captain Hank can explain the fight since I don't remember it. All I know is that when I woke up, we were in Ruld the port city HQ is stationed in, I had broken bones and felt horrible and Lucas was dead. I requested permission to learn dual welding swords as well as joining Captain Hank's crew. This is a trial basis, Captain Hank requested I join the crew since they were ordered escort duty here and he was short on fighting men."

"Why does Mason and Hank both make comment of you terrorizing cities and needing a sitter?" Dom asked leaning forward.

"The first island we landed, Eldridge our cook took a group to market to get provisions. Captain knew I had not been outside the kingdom so he assigned me to the landing party. I ate something that caused me to hallucinate to the point they had to take my weapons and lock me up when we got back to the ship. I also seem to find all the fights," Saber shrugged.

"So you have powers," another man murmured studying her, "Be honest because that's my power, to tell if someone is lying."

"I have powers although I didn't want any," Saber shrugged and met Axel's eyes, "Satisfied?"

"It explains a lot," Dom murmured, "I was shocked a navy girl wasn't complaining all morning."

"If you grew up the way I did, this morning was a cake walk," Saber met his gaze, "Now if you don't mind, I'd like to explore some more of your town before dark."

"You aren't asking any questions about us?" Axel asked her seriously.

"Admiral Oliver and Captain Hank said you were the best dual wielder they know. To be honest, I want to be stronger, past that I don't care much about your history or what you do."

"Admiral Oliver and Captain Hank think I'm going to join the Marines," Axel studied her, "To be frank, they don't pay crap and we can make more doing our own thing."

"Completely understandable," Saber shrugged, "I joined up because I was surrounded by nobility and military to the point that I'd be tossed in prison if I stepped a toe over the line. It was easier to join the Navy since I wanted to explore than to go about it any other way. Captain Hank's crew are known for being the wildest, more pirate-like crew in the fleet and I feel more at home with them than the prissy boys on the Admiral's deck."

Axel didn't smile, just studied her for a long moment. Dom asked one other question, "RNB...you said they weren't always bandits."

"You wouldn't find them in the history books because it was the biggest upset in the army's history," Saber reached up to tighten her ponytail and ignored the slight shift from one man on the far side of the room.

"Tell us," another man pressed.

"Ruld and Lidsing have been at war for decades. It is a mountainous border so there are only certain places to cross over. The army placed forts there to keep Lidsing out but there were a few places where they couldn't build defenses. Rumble was such a place, they assigned their best fighters to the border to protect it but year after year of turning the enemy away the army ordered the fighters, along with their families, to retreat to the fort which was a few miles inland. The Commander talked to the soldiers assigned to Rumble, he was a great tactician and explained that if they retreated it would give the enemy a bridgehead to get an army over the border which was what the enemy wanted but couldn't do since it was too mountainous. They decided as a unit to resign from the army and continue to protect their home. Because they resigned there were no supplies coming into the village so they had to go out and buy some, fighting meant they didn't make money so in hard times they had to steal. The army didn't assist them at all so they became a notorious bandit brigade that the army ignored, knowing that they had been wrong...a few years ago they were all massacred, it was reported no survivors and the army returned to Rumble to protect the border."

"You are all related to army soldiers who were protecting the border," Dom murmured softly.

"Yes, every man, woman, and child learned to fight because if you didn't you died. Part of our training was being tossed in the woods to survive for a few weeks and find our way back to the village. Sometimes tossed on the Lidsing side of the border to scout around for training with an older teen. Sometimes it worked and other times during training all of them died, it just depended on what trouble you found. Well am I going to disappear, Axel? I gave you my story."

"A story indeed but all true," the one with lie detector powers murmured.

"Very well, we will see you tomorrow at dawn," Axel agreed.

Dom flashed a smile, "You get to work with me again."

Saber nodded and turned to the door but Axel continued, "Being from a bandit community you know how to fight unarmed as well correct?"

She glanced back without turning toward him again and nodded once. Axel continued, "In return for training you, you will train someone I choose."

Saber shrugged slightly and said, "That's really up to my captain to decide. I just do what I'm told."

A door opened to the side and a teen came in and froze seeing her there. Saber turned to go as Axel glanced up at the teenager who hurried to whisper in his ear. Saber left without being stopped and slowly made her way through the markets and back toward the taverns and food vendors. She bought food and noticed two young children in rags in the street watching people pass. She bought extra food and had it wrapped in parchment paper to go. Meat was hard to come by if you lived in the city, hard to steal because it stayed on a grill while vegetables and fruits were easier. She bought a bag of three apples and took it to the two, passing them as she handed the bag to the little girl. The alley was dark but she didn't stop as she cut across to the next row of buildings. She made the mistake of coming to the pleasure district. The thoughts escalated into a roar in her mind and she sped up, cutting back to the food stalls. She paused in the alley to swipe her forehead before returning to the street beyond. She found Bradley sitting at a table outside a tavern with four others from the ship.

"Saber, how are you?" Bradley asked.

"Good now that I'm back over here," she sighed, "I made a wrong turn back a ways and it was too loud."

Being an officer, Bradley knew what she meant since her power was told to those of a certain rank. The others knew she could tell thoughts but weren't sure how or when. She was offered a seat but she shook her head, "I'm heading back to the ship, thanks though."

She left them still sitting at the table and moved back to the ship. She was right at the edge of the market when four individuals surrounded her, seeming not to care that the army guards from Ruld were sitting under canvas canopies watching the market for trouble. She had her journal tucked under her shirt in her waistband. She noticed the guards standing but instead of pulling swords the men attacked with fists. Saber defended, taking bruises without a word. The guards stepped forward to assist, tying the men up. "You will pay for getting our Cap'n arrested you wench."

"Can it," the corporal growled at them, "You picked this fight so you can go sit in timeout and answer to the justice system here for disturbing the peace."

Saber thanked them and kept moving, not noticing her shadows had moved closer to jump in if needed. She went to the ship and greeted Mason who touched her cheek, surprising her into stepping back. "You busted your lip and look like you had a tussle, what happened?"

"Nothing," Saber shook her head, "A group of four pirates thought jumping me in front of the army guards was a good idea. We had a fist fight and that was it."

"Same pirates that Robert ran into?" Mason folded his arms waiting. He was only four years older than her but over the past three months had settled into the authoritative role of first mate.

She saw his eyes and knew he wouldn't take a half answer, she sighed, "Yes sir, same ones."

"It's good to have Robert's back but if you mess with a crew they will find you again, don't leave the ship without someone to have your back, Saber, that's an order."

"Understood," she sighed.

"Tomorrow you are on watch over the ship," Mason informed her, "Four always stay on ship to guard it. Most work to fix things for our next journey out to sea but your job will be to man the plank."

"I can read while doing it?" Saber asked.

"Yes," he murmured, surprised she didn't complain. She nodded and went to her room, not seeing one of those shadowing her come up to the plank and talk to Mason. Hank tapped at her door and she answered it with book in hand, "Captain, what's up?"

"Axel paid me a visit in town," he studied her, "He said in return for training you, he wants you to train someone for him. I asked who it was and he said it was his younger cousin. I agreed after he explained why. It seems the kid is in some trouble in his home village and his family sent him to Axel."

"Trouble how?" Saber frowned.

"He refused to join a bandit brigade that is notorious for human trafficking. They try to recruit all the young men in the villages and it's a bad problem for them. Axel wants you to train him and stay with them for a few days at a time. I demanded a check in at least every two days and a report from you. I told him you have duties here tomorrow but after that you are released into his care. Don't break any laws and don't tell anyone outside of his group that you are navy—they know our crew are navy although we don't act like it. Understand?"

"Of course," Saber nodded.

"Get some rest," Hank murmured leaving.

The next day, Saber worked with Dom and read two books total as she sat on the plank that led to the dock, her crew had to step over her to enter or exit the ship so she didn't miss anyone. She wrote about the animals and when it was dark another four took over the watch for night shift. Saber packed her journal and a book along with two sets of clothes. Dom was there alone the next morning at dawn, Eldridge handed her a small satchel of food and looked to Dom, "This is only a snack so feed her right."

"Of course," Dom smirked, "For a rowdy bunch they sure like you, Barca."

"It's mutual," Saber continued walking, they left town, past the fighting ring the pirates used to gamble on fights and into the woods where a house and barn sat tucked into a meadow. Axel sat on the porch with a lanky brown-haired kid. Axel's gray eyes caught sight of Dom and Saber's arrival. He didn't move from the porch step as they walked up.

"Saber Barca this is Anthony Fields," Axel introduced. Saber offered a hand and Anthony didn't move.

"Why is a girl going to teach me how to fight unarmed, Axel?" Anthony frowned up at her, not reaching for her hand.

"You have bandit problems, right?" Saber asked him directly her hand dropping back to her side and watching his eyebrows shoot up as he nodded once, "Sometimes it's good to learn from someone who used to be a bandit. Yes a bandit from a different kingdom but a bandit none the less."

"You were a bandit?" Anthony scoffed, "You don't look like it."

Saber looked to Axel, "If I'm staying here for a few days at a time, where am I staying?"

Axel stood and turned to the house, "Follow me a moment."

They stepped around Anthony who openly thought it would be a waste of time to train with Saber. As Saber followed Axel in, Dom and Anthony stayed outside talking, "He thinks this is going to be a waste of time, Axel."

"I'm sure you will prove differently," Axel shrugged.

He showed her to a bedroom in the small three-bedroom cottage style house. Saber was shown around and found that there were cots in the barn. "Your friends stay here too?"

"It's safer than being spread out in town," Axel met her gaze, "It is mostly to protect you since Hank said if anything happens to you, we will wish we were never born. Evidently your foster father threatened his life if anything were to happen to his daughter."

"That Old Man sticks his nose into everything," Saber muttered, she was surprised to find she actually missed him and Giselle though.

They went back out to find a few others on the porch talking and relaxing. Saber found Dom turning to her, "Of a morning you will train and after that Anthony is all yours."

Saber nodded once as Axel returned to the porch. She practiced with Dom, they had advanced quickly to fighting together. It was sequences but Dom would throw in an extra swipe at her. She was good at catching it. She didn't say a word as she sweat freely all morning. Dom had her fighting against others who didn't use the sequences and she sometimes had to jump out of the way if she couldn't block it, each time Dom would tell her how to fix the problem. Mostly it was holding her blades too low or at odd angles that created openings.

When it was lunch a guy with fire red hair called it was time for food, they sat around the porch and ate. Saber froze on the first bite, it was amazing food, she looked up at the red head, "You made this?"

He grinned, "Part of my power is increasing ingredients to make it taste great but also give the best nutrients to the eaters."

"I've ate with all kinds of different people, even nobility and never once ate something this good," she murmured to herself.

"I'm glad you like it," he grinned.

Saber ate the rest of her food in silence and rested for a moment before looking at Anthony who just finished. She gave him half an hour to let his food settle before pulling him into the shady part of the yard. The men sat on the porch watching her. She told him to attack her but when she said to stop, he would stop. Anthony agreed with a frown.

Saber watched him, she could tell he was learning to fight with a sword since he had balance and didn't over reach but had a lot of openings. She nodded to herself and said, "Stop."

He stepped back, well aware she hadn't moved a single step forward or back as they fought. He was thinner than she'd like but with the red head's cooking that would be fixed soon. Saber did push ups with him, to start they would do 50. Anthony struggled to follow her orders as he sunk lower. She then showed him balancing techniques such as hand stands and one handed ones at that.

"What's this do?"

"The more familiar you are with your center of gravity and balance the better you can fight. It also works your muscles differently than any other exercise," Saber said going into a one-handed stand to reach her shirt which was sliding up to her breastband, she tucked it in and walked forward a few steps before tucking her feet and rolling back to stand facing him. She turned to Axel, "We need a place to run for Anthony here. At least a mile or two each day."

"Consider it done," Axel studied her.

"Alright," she faced Anthony again, "Now, I need two volunteers."

The men looked at each other and the cook and another came forward. Saber nodded, one was about her size in height and the other was taller. She looked at the cook, "Get me in a headlock."

He moved behind her, being taller and she warned, "Bandits play dirty so not every fist fight stays a fist fight. What's your name, chef?"

"Everyone calls me Red, but my real name is Henry," he murmured asking if she were ready.

"Anthony, watch everything, he's going to choke me out for real and I'm going to get out of it," she murmured.

"Okay," Anthony stood at an angle to them both to watch.

Red choked her for real, Saber reached for his arm and grabbed a pressure point. Red grit his teeth and tightened his hold. Saber swung her elbow back to nail his ribs and he loosened his grip enough for her to get out of it. She stopped with her hand still holding the pressure point but she let it go.

"You didn't try to pull him off of you, why?" Anthony cocked his head.

"He's stronger than me, when you are up against someone stronger, you have to fight smarter. Think through what you know and plan ahead. That was a pressure hold, against an enemy instead of aiming for their ribs which may or may not work, you aim for the family jewels. If they complain about it, only amateurs get hit so they can suck it up. Different techniques work for different situations. You could even use a knife to stab if you can't get free. Red here is taller than me, so I used that hold. However...ah...what's your name?"

"Samuel," the other murmured.

"Samuel is about the same height as I am, so fighting him will be different because the hold and angles are different," Saber explained more on holds. Anthony winced when she grabbed the pressure point on his hand and squeezed gently. He would remember it, she taught him a lot in a single day. She even showed how to choke out someone herself. She did Samuel first and surprised all of them with leaning back.

"Getting your opponent off balance can surprise them into what my family calls blanking—they panic to the point they can't think of a way out of the hold," Saber said as Samuel tapped her arm, since he wasn't supposed to fight her just yet. She let him go and he rubbed his neck in surprise.

"Now Red is a different story," she looked up at the cook who was watching her. She continued, "First off to reach his neck is going to take a certain level of surprise or using your wits to get there. He's tall enough I can't reach easily so if you use surprise then you can do this."

She took a running start at Red who was told not to move, she used a tree to help her jump up, she slipped her arm around his throat as her legs locked around his waist, she didn't tighten although Red took two steps to balance himself from her knocking into his back. "The problem with this is if there are trees or anything for him to slam back into, you will get pummeled but it's harder to get away from me because I'm locked in with my legs."

Red's face was turning red and he asked, "What's the best way to get out of it then?"

"Find something to slam me into, knock the air out of my lungs and my grip will loosen, if you tighten your neck muscles in time you will have more time to reach down and unhook my ankles."

He reached down and grabbed her boots, unhooking her ankles and pulling her off. Saber landed on her feet when Red turned around.

"You want to get your opponent dazed so they land in a heap and can't attack you again," Saber told them.

Anthony worked on different holds, fighting against them as well as trying them out. Red glanced up at the sun and said, "I need to start cooking."

"Thanks for your help," Saber nodded as Samuel continued learning with Anthony. Saber stopped them both and told them to stretch out. She walked them through stretches that would help keep them limber and cool down their muscles. When they finished, Red called food and they sat together with the others on the porch. The other guys studied Saber in surprise.

"So who taught you to fight, Saber?" Anthony asked her seriously.

"My brothers," she smirked, "And they were about a thousand times harder on me than anyone else I've trained under."

"How far apart are you from them?" Anthony asked.

Saber thought back to those days and found all of them watching her, not all of them were there when Axel questioned her, "I'm a year and a half younger than Delta, three years younger than Charlie, five years younger than Bravo, and eight years younger than Ace...Ace never trained me, he was stolen from us just before I was born but the others were hard on me. They said they had to make sure I was the toughest out of the family or I'd be hurt and they couldn't have that."

"Where are they now?" Anthony asked, thinking of his family and how they were very similar.

Saber shook her head with a smirk meeting his eyes, "Right now, resting."

Axel studied her, she didn't tell Anthony her entire village was massacred because he was currently worried about his own village. Saber looked to Dom, "Captain Hank said you were to take reports to him if I wasn't going back to the ship. Do you have paper?"

"Yes," Dom nodded.

She wrote quickly and set the pen down, leaving it open as she went to shower. Axel didn't care if they judged him, he read her report and was surprised at what she wrote, she planned to train Anthony in more than hand to hand fighting it seemed. He handed it to Dom who read it as well and raised a surprised eyebrow.

"Hey Axel?" Anthony asked as everyone relaxed on the porch.

"What's up?" Axel looked at him, Dom made orders for one of their runners to take it to Hank or whoever was on the ship.

"How does a bandit from a different country get here?" Anthony asked curiously.

"That is her story to tell," Axel shook his head, "She's a talented fighter so I want you all to learn all you can while she's here. She won't be here for long."

"Okay," Anthony could see the logic, if Axel said she was talented it meant he saw her as an equal.

Saber came back out in loose clothes and wet hair that she braided out of her way. She sat with them and said, "Tell me about your kingdom. I want to learn more about it."

"What would you like to know?" Axel studied her, wondering why she cared to know.

"Is it the only one on this land or are there other kingdoms?" Saber asked watching him.

"There are seven others, three of which share borders with us," Dom murmured.

"Oh right, I meant to ask, do you have ticks here? I didn't find any but being in the woods at home, you had to be careful so I want to make sure," Saber shook her head, realizing she was getting ahead of herself.

"What are ticks?" Anthony frowned confused.

"Little bloodsuckers with six legs. They are about the size of an ant from what I read in the insect books I got from the vendor."

"We do not have those, and good thing too, I do not think I would like the woods much if there were ticks," Red shook his head.

They talked until late, Saber asking a million questions, the guys were interested in her as well and asked a lot about Ruld which she answered without hesitation. A few weeks passed, she ended up fighting with all of them, Axel still refused to fight her although she didn't ask him to fight her either. She learned a lot, they could see her technique changing before their eyes.

Chapter 3

"Where's Red? I'm starving!" Anthony collapsed on the porch after the training with Saber. It was nearly supper time, Saber had been putting them through their paces, the whole group had been through the ringer. All except for Axel who studied her quietly from the porch, working on paperwork or talking to messengers. He trained somewhere else after supper or before dawn, she wasn't sure.

"He's not back from his errand," Dom frowned, "He probably won't want to cook when he gets back either."

"Then who's cooking?" Anthony sighed.

"Red nearly killed Dom for touching his stuff the last time," Samuel shook his head, "I'm not risking his wrath."

"He won't kill me, I'm craving something and I'll just whip it up if you don't mind eating Delight and I'm allowed to borrow your kitchen?" Saber shocked them when she asked Axel directly, the first question since she arrived. He only nodded when everyone looked at him.

Saber searched the cabinets before starting. She pulled things out that she needed and cleaned as she went. She made a huge meal for everyone and felt eyes on her back from those sitting on the patio. As she cooked, she heard Red's thoughts, *if that kitchen is trashed I don't care if she is a girl.*

"Calm down, Red," she didn't turn to look at him when he stopped in the hall. She was aware there were others behind him watching how it might play out. Red stepped into the kitchen, "Whoa that smells amazing!"

"You didn't have all the ingredients but it'll do," Saber muttered.

"I expected a disaster since I was running late," Red sighed.

"Well they were starving and I was craving this so I asked if they minded, I didn't want them to drop from hunger."

Saber let him help her pack everything outside. After the meal not a crumb was left. Red asked for the recipe and Saber smirked, "It's a well-guarded secret of my family."

"Please?"

"Have you earned it?" Saber asked.

Red froze thinking about how she might mean that question. "How do you mean?"

"How about this, you can fight me for it. Your choice of weapons or hand-to-hand. You land a decisive blow and you win. You can wait or try as many times as you want but I leave in two weeks. Cap'n Hank just announced it when I went back to report in."

"Any time?" Red frowned, he hated fighting but Axel told him to train with her.

"No surprise attacks, you have to announce your intention," Saber knew he really wanted the recipe, he was a chef that valued recipes and willing to fight for them.

"She had a rough day, try her now, Red. I want you to make this again," Dom smiled.

"One more thing," Saber raised a finger, "I decide if you've earned it if you can land a blow."

"Now," Red murmured, maybe he could win now and then he wouldn't have to hit her again. He didn't believe it was polite to hit a girl and it was really uncomfortable for him to train and fight her. Saber nodded, standing.

"With what exactly?" Saber asked.

"Hand-to-hand," red struggled with hand to hand but didn't want to hurt her with a weapon.

He lost, Saber gave a ten minute time limit. Every few hours Red tried when he was there. Axel sent him to check on things when Saber went to the ship to report in. They were about to go into the woods for her to train on tracking and hunting. They were all going and camping out since Hank gave approval.

When Saber got back to the meadow, she found a scene that reminded her of a kicked bee hive. She came forward looking around, "Where is Anthony?"

"He overheard Red's report," Axel met her gaze, "His village was attacked and younger brother was taken. His mom was roughed up. Go back to the ship, we can't have you coming with us being Navy and all."

Saber tightened her satchel on her back, "It's a good thing I don't have to report for a week. I can't miss my ship but I can help until then."

Axel had turned away from her but when she said that he turned, "Navy will frown on that."

"I'm teaching you to track and fight. You are teaching me dual sword. I don't need to describe the tracks."

"Thanks, Saber," he murmured.

"Bring clothes that will camouflage to the surroundings," Saber called to everyone packing in the shed before looking at Dom who studied her in surprise, "When did he leave?"

"Early this morning. We thought he was in town but found a message."

"We leave in five minutes!" Axel told them. Red had people helping him pack supplies but Saber took over, "We'll get vegetables in the woods and hunt if we need it."

Red agreed seeing her book on plants, he knew most edible as well. Saber found the deer trail that Anthony used and jogged while looking for signs. It was nearly breakfast so he had just a few hours head start.

"Is this a straight shot to the village?"

"Yes, this trail goes straight there."

"Forget tracking then, lets catch up to him and then track these idiots."

"Sounds good," Axel nodded and they kept up with her. Her pace was harsh but kept them eating miles without losing steam. They got to the village close to noon and found Anthony with his family. He was about to leave and started arguing with Axel. Saber irritated hit Anthony in the back of the head and met his gaze, "Would you listen? Get clothes for the situation. You are wasting time. If they took people they'll be slow."

Anthony stared in shock but Red rushed him to his house. Saber asked, "How long ago did it happen?"

"Night before last," Anthony's mom murmured, "They left late yesterday afternoon with fifty kids, livestock and our valuables."

"Wagons or walking?" Saber was devoid of emotion. The crew of Axel's were surprised.

"They stole two wagons for the valuables but no animals to pull it so they were having the ones stolen pull it."

"They mention where they are headed or who's the buyer?"

"They were heading to their hideout in Skull Cavern to the North, then to an auction house in Buta."

"Got a map?" Saber asked Axel but the village headman gave it to her. Red gave her a steamed bun filled with hot meat.

"They would've stopped at nightfall or risk losing hostages, probably here," Saber muttered to herself, "They will struggle here since teens are pulling wagons, that is if the creek is up."

"In the crossing it's chest deep but it was flooding because of all the rain three nights ago and still rising."

Saber used her finger to measure and looked to the villagers asking more questions as Axel talked to his aunt for a moment. When she finished she looked to Axel, "I'm ready whenever you are, we should just be able to cut them off before the creek."

"Saddle up boys," Axel called. Saber ate the bun and asked to keep the map, the village headman nodded without saying a word. She tightened her hair, holding the last two bites of the bun in her mouth. She tucked the map in her pack and led them into the woods at a jog, they kept up but Anthony asked why through the woods.

Saber growled to be quiet as she explained it was a shortcut. They raced through the woods. The road snaked back on itself over and over. Each time Saber would pause and check the road and explained the tracks before they raced through the woods again. They reached the creek knowing they were ahead of the bandits. They used the time to rest, it would be a rough fight since they had more bandits than Axel had men. The villagers estimated forty bandits to Axels fifteen. Saber looked to Axel, "The question is how are we getting everything back to the village when I wasn't planning to feed over sixty people."

"We have to fight them first then worry about feeding the kids," Axel shook his head.

"True," Dom nodded.

Saber stretched and stood, "I'll be back."

"Where are you heading?" Dom frowned.

"Looking to see how long of a wait we have," she muttered.

"I'm going with you, maybe we can dwindle their numbers," Axel murmured, "Dom you stay here and prepare the men."

"Sir," Dom nodded.

Axel called two others and the four of them took off across to the other side of the road. Saber told them to watch their step, they needed to be as silent as ever. They found the group coming around the final turn, Saber took them farther into the woods and around to the back. She stopped and looked to Axel who studied her, "I'm a coastal guy, you take the lead, Saber."

"Okay," she whispered, "We are going to hit and run, fight fast and try to draw your opponent to the woods. Don't pull too many or we won't be able to do it again."

They attacked the end of the line and retreated quickly before they could report on their numbers. They successfully hit them and retreated without the entire line knowing about it. They did it again, they ended up killing eighteen before the bandits realized what was going on. Saber told them to retreat back toward the woods where the rest were located. They attacked the other side of the line and ran. They had pulled too many this time but Saber had led them directly to their friends. They stepped out of the woods just before the creek and faced the enemy, the kids were chained to the wagons pulling them but seeing their way blocked, they stopped and sat exhausted.

Saber saw Red lose his sword and before she could react, Red pulled a throw she had just taught him the day before. She focused back on her own fight and when she was free again, she looked around to see that the bandits were nearly completely wiped out. Dom had the bandits that gave up drag the dead to the woods to rot. They didn't have time to dig graves since they didn't have shovels. Anthony and Samuel unlocked the chains from the kids and chained the bandits to the wagon. They were going to be pulling the wagons back to the village they stole from. Anthony came up to Axel frowning, "He's not here, Axel, my brother is still missing."

"Anthony, Bentley was taken with a group of six ahead on horseback since he was fighting so much," another teen told him looking beat up.

"Did they have any others that separated from the group? No one else left between here and your village right?"

"No all the others chased after you earlier when you attacked," the boy murmured.

"Anthony help take all these guys home with the rest of the crew. Lagoon, Pierce, come with us. Saber can you help us track them down?"

"We need faster rides than just running through the woods. Not to mention that Red will need help getting these guys food if they hope to make it back to the village without collapsing."

"We are good on the food front," Red corrected, "They have food in one of the wagons to feed everyone. We have enough to get these kids home at least."

"Get them home, if you run into any of Saber's crew don't tell them anything, understand?"

"Sure," Dom agreed.

Saber nodded once and pulled her weapons off and slowly made her way across what she considered a river since it was so high. She held her weapons and personal belongings out of the water and looked along the bank and referenced the map the villagers gave her.

"If they are heading to the Buta, we need to aim for this point here," Saber looked up to Axel who watched her look at the map, "Their base is one way and Buta is the other so getting to the crossing will help us decide which way to go. No other villages are around this area so it should be easy to find since their horses have unique shoes on."

Axel looked at the mark in the mud, it had an SS imprint in the nails that held the shoes in place. She led them straight, this road zig and zagged too but it was straight for at least a mile. Pierce said, "That kid said they left the group at around noon when Bentley fought one too many times. They aren't more than a few hours."

"Let's just hope we can make it to the crossing before we lose the light," Saber muttered.

They knew it was time sensitive, they raced through the woods. Just as the sun was dying on the horizon, they finally made it to the crossing. She looked at each side, it had rained a lot but the prints were fresh heading to Buta. Saber cursed softly and looked at the group following her.

"Buta it is," Axel nodded, "We can follow the road for a few more hours, the village is only about six miles more."

"Alright," Saber nodded, "You're the boss."

"We don't know when he's being sold," Axel murmured, "I'd wait as well but we need to figure out what they are doing."

She nodded and led them on, the woods sounded exactly the same as home which was comforting. She mumbled, "I want a horse to ride back, we might need to skedaddle quick anyway."

"We'll deal with that when we get to it, Saber," Axel growled.

"Just making sure you remember the finer points mister coastal guy."

The village was lit up and Saber did the talking asking about an inn. There were two in the village. She noticed a tattoo on the one guard's neck and murmured, "Any auctions going on in the next few days?"

"What?" he growled.

It was dark enough that she knew he wouldn't be able to clearly see her tattoo, she turned and flashed her tattoo and he straightened in surprise, "Yes ma'am, where you from?"

"Slaver ship in need of more oarsmen," she muttered, "Too many Marines at the port so I came inland with a few of my boys to replace the ones we lost."

"I see," he nodded, "The auction is in three days. Most of the people coming for the auction are staying at the inn called Brigade, the auction will be in the stable yard."

"Thanks friend," Saber glanced to Axel, "Tip the man."

Axel gave him enough to buy a beer and walked on without a word. Saber sighed, "I want a shower and we were in luck that it's dark out."

"True," Axel admitted, "Glad you came after all."

Saber mentally touched wood in case their luck took a turn for the worst. She led them to the inn and asked for two rooms. The innkeeper didn't bat an eye, they got into the rooms, Axel paid again, and Saber took a shower. The rooms connected on the balconies so they were together without being together. Axel was sitting in her room when she got out of the shower in loose clothes.

"We are roommates for the night, here's your food, we already ate," he muttered.

"Thanks," she frowned sitting to eat. She glanced at him, he had laid back to stare at the ceiling, seemingly deep in thought.

"You ever been here before, Axel?" she asked seriously after finishing the hot meal.

"No," he shook his head.

"Okay," she nodded, "You get some sleep, I'll be back in a bit."

She grabbed her satchel and pulled a rope out of it. They were on the second floor and the windows below them were shuttered and dark for the night. Saber surprised him with tying the rope off and slipping over the side. "What the hell are you doing?"

"Checking the stable to see if they are staying here. Also snooping in the stable for any hidden holding areas. If I can find where they are being held, the sooner we can get out of here."

"Sure," he muttered, "And if you are caught you are dead."

"Ye of little faith," she dropped out of sight and he cursed, he didn't even see her get to the stable. He sat up waiting, wondering if he shouldn't have went with her.

Being late it was easier for her to move around, Saber could hear their thoughts but couldn't figure out how to get to them. She pinpointed where the sound was the loudest, somehow they were in the stable yard underground. She wasn't sure where the way down was located. She searched the stable top to bottom in the dark but didn't find anything.

She did find the horses that they were chasing. She went back up just before dawn and found Axel fighting sleep as she crawled back up to the balcony and untied the rope, stowing it again as she came inside. She was exhausted. She laid down on the second bed facing Axel with a huge yawn.

"Stable had the horses we were chasing. I hear thoughts in the stable yard but they are muffled like they are behind a wall which if they are underground it would make sense. As for finding a way to them, I looked everywhere in the yard and stable, no dice. I found a cellar in the inn but couldn't get into it because the cooks were blocking the door."

"Could you identify anyone?" he asked.

"No," she shook her head.

"Let's just hope the rumors are false," Axel whispered lying flat again.

"What rumors?" Saber curled into a ball ignoring that she still had her boots and weapons on.

"A rumor that the bandits have a king in our kingdom. He fought all the bandit groups and won against their leaders. Instead of killing them all off they are his subordinates."

Saber was already fast asleep, Axel was surprised she hadn't passed out from all the running from the day. They had five days to get back to the port for her to get her ship, hopefully she could teach them how to track and hunt before then. He mentally crossed his fingers before sleep took him as well. The next day they went down and had breakfast, Saber still half asleep but alert. They ate in silence, watching the room however the room was boisterous as any place with a lot of bandits.

"Excuse me, lovely lady, which group are you with?" a smooth voice asked. Saber turned slightly and glanced up to see a man around 20 years old in a black cloak studying her.

"Who are you?" she asked back.

"He's the Bandit King, watch your tone wench!" a man growled from the table behind him.

"Enough, Winston," he murmured, "I would remember you if you were in a bandit group."

"Why do you assume I'm with a bandit group," she asked curiously.

"The way you hold yourself, these guys are similar but you act like a bandit leader," he pulled a chair from a different table to Saber's table.

"You wound me," Saber touched her chest, his eyes tracked her hand and she heard an idol thought from Pierce of attacking. She leaned forward to grab her drink and murmured, "Don't move boys."

"So what's your name?" the Bandit King asked.

"You first, I'm not just going to call you king after all," she smirked.

"Call me Ethan," he chuckled, "So?"

"Saber," she watched him, her smile faded, "To be clear, I dated a bandit from here, I'm from Ruld. Our ship hold slaves and we lost a few in a storm and I remembered being told auctions were held every once in a while. I brought the boys here to see if we could get our hands on a few."

"A bandit at sea?" Ethan shook his head, "Prove it, Saber."

She didn't move but studied him, "Middle of my back."

Ethan reached for her shirt and lifted it, everyone in the room was silent as he did. Her tattoo was elaborate in colored ink, showing she was the leader or part of the leader's family. "So why were you at sea?"

"That's my business," she smiled as he pulled her shirt back down.

"Clear the room," Ethan ordered, "Your goons too or I'll kill them."

"Go," Saber met Axel's eyes calmly. When everyone was gone, Ethan leaned back studying her.

"Why do I have a feeling you are lying to me?" he asked, eyes searching her face. Saber's poker face was top notch so she didn't worry.

"I'm searching for one of our own that was stolen a while back," Saber met his gaze, "He's not here but I made a few friends and one's younger brother was taken for an auction. They aren't bandits just normal civilians, they asked for my help. I've never heard of a bandit king, you are the first...listen I'm willing to pay for the kid but I don't want to wait around forever. I have places to go myself."

"Bandits are invited to this inn only if they fall under my banner," Ethan studied her, "So come to the stable yard, if you win I'll let you look through the people being held here. If you lose, you stay with me."

"To be honest we stole people to join our group we never dealt in human trafficking, I don't like it and I don't think you would want me to stay here either, Ethan."

Ethan grinned and motioned, "Stable yard, no excuses."

She led him outside, putting her hair in a ponytail and turning to face him, she had her swords but he told her they were fighting unarmed. She noticed he didn't have weapons on him that she could tell. She glanced up at the balcony to find Pierce, Lagoon and Axel there staring at her. She pulled her weapons and tossed them up, "Keep ahold of them for me."

"Saber," Axel started but she raised her hand and he stopped talking.

Ethan attacked without warning and she dodged his initial two attacks before getting slammed in the side with a surprise kick. She winced as her ribs groaned. He was powerful, more so than he looked, she fought back, using every trick in the book and then some. She yanked him off his feet and landed on his chest with her fist back, "Yield?"

"No," he flipped her over his head and she tucked and rolled back up, turning just in time to avoid a fist to the face. She frowned at him and cracked a joke.

"Watch the face, that's my best feature!"

Ethan chuckled but continued to fight hard. Saber was trembling as the fight continued, she used forms and fighting techniques that her brothers showed her from other bandit clans, she even used techniques from the hand to hand fighters that the Old Man hired. Ethan took a few hits and was bleeding same as her, she braced her hands on her knees breathing fast, "Why are we fighting again? I think I forgot."

"I want to see how I stack up against a different kingdom, it would be cool to be the bandit king of the known world after all," Ethan grinned not caring that every balcony was full. Saber met his gaze, swaying just enough to miss the next attack.

"How about this, I acknowledge you are king of the bandits but I still go free and you let me sneak peak the slaves?" Saber had an eye shut, she had missed an attack and blood was running into her eye.

"Two more good hits and you'll be out so why bargain?" Ethan grinned.

"I'm not one to give in to anyone's whims," Saber stood still breathing fast but reached up as she held Ethan's gaze as she swiped the blood from her eye. He attacked fast and hard but she went just as hard, he landed with her in a choke hold. Saber hit the pressure point but it didn't work, she tried tossing him over her shoulder but his body was built like a mountain. She kicked back, hitting him in the privates and he grunted in pain. She slipped out of his grasp and faced him again.

He punched her hard in the face, she spit blood, her eye swelling although she could still see out of it. She ducked under his next left hook and hit him solidly in the gut, following up with an uppercut. He staggered back and she heard a stray thought, *Dang she's good. I know how she fights now, I'm good.*

Ethan held out a hand and she studied him, "No funny business right?"

"None at all," he agreed, "You want to see the slaves as your reward correct?"

"Yes," she nodded and hesitated for only a second more, again his thoughts slipping into her mind in the sea of shock from the others watching, *Agree, it's not every day I find someone who can keep up with me, beautiful.*

She accepted his hand and shook it, she let go just as quickly and looked up at the boys she came with and nodded to Axel, "Come here, Ax."

He had her swords and jumped down, handing them back to her and watching Ethan curiously. "Ax, huh?"

"I'm Axel," Axel offered a hand.

"Ethan," the King greeted, "Your lady here is a great fighter."

Axel nodded and they were led to the underground holding pen. Saber swiped her face as Axel walked through. No one else was down there and every thought was laced with fear at being sold, all that was except for one that sounded faint, *Axel? Am I dreaming?*

Saber stepped past Axel who was slowly walking and continued forward looking around. She found a boy of around 15 leaning against the cell wall staring blearily out toward Axel. She squatted to look into the cell better and asked, "You Bentley?"

"Yeah," he agreed surprised.

"Axel," Saber reached into the bars and touched the boy's forehead.

Axel turned on Ethan, "How much for the kid?"

"He's family, I take it?"

"Bandits killed twenty villagers," Axel turned to him not admitting anything.

"He has a high fever," Saber murmured looking him over, "He needs a healer."

"Three gold," Ethan told her.

"He won't last the night and you think he'd make that much at auction?" Saber glared at him. Axel looked down in frustration, *I don't have that much.*

"Fine two, he has potential," Ethan crossed his arms.

"1 and four silver," Saber tried.

Ethan shook his head, "Two or you can wait for the auction."

"Throw in a healer to look at his wounds and clear him to travel then you have a deal," Saber muttered.

"Deal," Ethan nodded stepping forward and touching the kid, his cuts and bruises disappeared like they had never been there. Bentley stared in surprise. Ethan turned to Saber who stood and pulled two gold out of her purse at her hip. He shocked her with kissing her gently. *Can't pass up kissing a beautiful lady like her.*

She felt his power radiate down healing everything from the cracked ribs to the swollen eye. She stepped back staring at him, "Do that again and the fight will be with swords and to the death, understand me?"

Ethan grinned accepting the money and unlocking the door for Bentley to get out. Saber looked to Axel who studied Ethan and her in surprise, "Tie the kid up so it looks as though he's our slave, Ax."

"Right," Axel tied Bentley and Saber looked up at Ethan, "Any horse flesh for sell?"

"Only four," Ethan shook his head, "Twenty silver."

Saber knew he was charging nearly quadruple the amount that would be standard, pulled her purse from her breastband and handed over the right amount, she stuffed it back under his watchful eyes. She looked at the boys, "Go get the others and our gear, meet me in the stable. Anyone to stop you, kill them, I'm tired of playing around."

"Yes ma'am," Axel didn't try to establish he was the leader, bandits were her forte so he let her lead to keep them from a war. Ethan glanced at her as they started back up the stairs, "You really came all this way for one boy?"

"I owed a debt, it's paid," Saber nodded, "Where are the horses?"

Ethan helped her saddle the horses as they talked, the inn was silent, tense since the king showed up. He told her that he was trying to get them to stop human trafficking but it was survival for them since it was a poor kingdom with a king who demanded high taxes on everyone. She met his gaze as the others came and got on the horses. Lagoon had her satchel and tied it to one of the horses, "You have a bandit group that stays around here in the caverns. Make sure they don't take their anger out on the village toward the port city, I'm the one that attacked their brothers and released the fifty children they planned to sell. If they have a problem with that, they can find me at the port for a week more."

"How many did your small group here take on?"

"Did we get a count?" Saber asked the others.

"Forty-three," Lagoon answered.

Saber got on and helped Bentley on behind her, "I don't like trafficking and most the children were younger than ten. You have your work cut out for you, Bandit King, and I wish you luck."

"If you come back to our kingdom, look me up, Saber."

She smirked, "I'll think about it."

They rode out quickly with Saber leading. Bentley held onto her tight, never having rode a horse correctly before since the last time they tied him on the horse like a sack of feed. Axel and his guys were better but not by much. They were quiet as they rode, only taking breaks to eat and use the restroom since Pierce had bought bread and jerky from Buta. Saber didn't say much although Axel tried to thank her.

"We have four days to train your men and then I'm on a ship out of here," she met his gaze.

"Who are you?" Bentley asked confused still riding with her since she was the lightest of the group to help the horse not tire so quickly.

"Saber Barca, a former bandit from Ruld," she muttered.

"How do you know Axel?" Bentley was confused.

"She's the one that has been teaching Anthony," Axel told him.

They got him home late that night, they stayed in a barn with the rest of Axel's crew. Saber took a shower in the house and came out feeling human again, they went to the woods and she taught them everything she could in the time left. They took her to the dock the morning the ship was to leave and Saber handed Red a small packet of papers, he frowned opening it to find recipes.

"But…I didn't win."

"I saw you fighting the bandits," she murmured quietly, "You used techniques you just learned. You deserve these. Next time we meet, you can cook these for me."

"I owe you, Saber," Axel met her gaze, "I'll pay that debt."

"Stay out of trouble," she shook his hand, "You don't owe me anything, you trained me like you promised and I'm thankful."

She waved and ran up to the ship where the crew greeted her with a cheer. They watched as the three ships backed slowly out of the harbor, Saber stood in the stern and waved to them as they left. Axel murmured, "She's worth her weight in gold."

Saber wasn't surprised that Hank set a hand on her shoulder, "How'd the training go?"

"Great," she murmured, "I fought with a lot of different people and picked up a few new techniques for hand to hand, knife and swords."

"Good," he murmured.

Downside was she was completely out of money, her reward for the bounty hadn't come in yet but she had received five gold from the navy as a reward for her hard work. She had kept three back home in a bank so she had a little savings but the rest of her money was gone, she had three silver left until they were paid for this voyage. They ran across pirates on four different occasions and Saber fought like a wildfire. Mason was shocked at the way she fought now, it was completely unrecognizable from before, and Hank agreed with him.

As they neared HQ Port, Ruld, Mason asked him, "Can we make her the Udan?"

"Really, Mason?" Hank frowned watching her training with the men, she was walking them through hand to hand, teaching them more than they would have ever learned in the boot camp.

"First Mate and Helmsman is a lot for one person. Udan is used to alleviate the pressure," Mason shrugged, "It's a Ruld pirating term but she would be in charge of commanding the landing crews, she has the knowledge where I'm lacking."

"We will see what Admiral Oliver says about keeping her on. I won't use that term but will ask for an elevation of her rank through a trial."

"Good," Mason nodded.

Saber went home to visit Giselle and the Old Man, they asked about her trip, she brought her books home for Giselle to read and kept her journal which had just as much information about the different plants and what was edible on her trip. Red gave her a few recipes to try and she had shared them with Eldridge. She went to eat with them and talked about eating the fruit and vegetable by accident, Giselle was surprised but Ulric asked what her power was. She explained it and he frowned.

"So you know what everyone is thinking?" he pressed.

"No it's only in certain situations like wishing for someone to help or aimed at someone else, I can hear that," she shrugged.

Like this, Saber? His voice sounded slightly different and she nodded once as she wondered why his thoughts sounded different, younger even.

"Excuse me," a messenger for the Admiral appeared at Saber's elbow, "Admiral Oliver requests your presence immediately."

She grabbed the roll and sandwich and flashed an amused smile at Giselle who said it was rude to eat and walk, "Orders, Auntie."

She ate as she followed the messenger and found Hank, Mason, Admiral Oliver and James were sitting at a table. She still had the bread roll in one hand and saluted hoping they wouldn't notice. Of course Hank noticed, "At ease, finish your roll, Lieutenant Barca."

"Sorry sir, was having a family meal when I was summoned," Saber apologized.

"Tomorrow at dawn you will be tested against James and two other top brass to test your fighting skills. You can fight with dual swords but they will be wooden so no injuries. If you pass you will be assigned to Captain Hank's ship moving forward and will leave the day after tomorrow."

"Yes sir," she nodded.

"How was your training?"

"Good sir, I learned a lot about the kingdom as well as the weapons."

"What did you learn that peaked your interest?" Oliver asked watching her.

"They have a Bandit King for one," she murmured, "From what I heard he's ambitious. They have a lot of different plant life and animals, Axel's friend Red gave me recipes which I shared with Eldridge. At the end of the training I also heard comment from Dom that they may not be joining the Navy, sir."

"Really?" Oliver frowned, "Then we will just have to hope they don't become pirates and attack our ships."

"Agreed," Hank sighed, "I wondered when they were hanging around the shady part of the port with pirates."

Saber answered more questions, avoiding the bandit fight and kidnapping, then she went back through the market to get some food. She made it home and spent the evening relaxing with Ulric and Giselle.

The next morning she reported to HQ training yard where both crews appeared to want to watch her test. She glanced around with a frown, "Nothing better to do while we are in port?"

"Not a thing," Mason grinned.

She sighed as James came out and tossed her two wooden swords. She was in her uniform since she was being tested. She fought hard and shocked everyone with winning against James. She glanced up as she helped James to his feet, Oliver summoned another to test her as James went to his seat. She noticed fresh recruits had joined sometime during the fight. Quartermaster of HQ was second in command of the Navy for Ruld. He was known for being strong, Oliver gave a time limit and asked someone to keep time. Saber stretched for a second as the Quartermaster came out and launched a surprise attack.

Saber just barely dodged it, she was quick on her feet but he was lethal even with a sword. She held her own but it was touch and go, she would have gave up if it had been just a training but because her life on Hank's ship rode on the outcome she pushed harder. She incorporated moves from hand to hand in with her attacks and surprised him but it didn't matter. Before she threw caution to the wind and played dirty, a yell of 'TIME' caused them both to pause.

"I've never seen a fighting style like that, Lieutenant Barca, well done," he murmured as he walked away.

"Thank you sir," she was sweating buckets and decided she needed a drink, she looked around and caught Lincoln's eyes, "Toss me your canteen, Linc."

He didn't bat an eye at the order, he tossed it to her and she drank for a second before hearing Oliver calling out another of HQ's top brass, this one was known for the most lethal in fighting, even more so than the Quartermaster. She noticed he was bare handed and she tossed the two wooden swords to Linc along with his water. She moved back to the middle and prepared mentally for a beating. He was known for fighting without pause or care for rules. Saber held a loose stance watching him, swiping sweat from her brow without taking her eyes off him.

"Five minutes, if you are still standing you have accomplished your test, Lieutenant Barca," Oliver murmured, "For those watching who are not part of a ship, this is a rare test specifically for Barca to advance rank as requested with Captain Hank and his crew. Take note because you are witnessing some of the Navy's best fighters on display today. Now....Begin!"

Saber moved just enough that he grazed her side but didn't hit, kicking as hard as she could into his side. He caught her leg and flung her to the ground. She snapped around, gritting her teeth as she wrestled to get free. She was taking a one-sided beating but she was learning from him, trying to dodge the worst but gaining a swollen eye and cracked ribs anyway. He decked her again and Saber knew she wasn't out for the count, fighting unconsciousness as she staggered to her feet again.

"Give it up girl, you are no match for me," he growled.

"I'm not done yet," she didn't care if she was disciplined for fighting as if her life depended on it, anything less than killing him was acceptable in her mind. She took hit after hit but she was giving just as good as she got. It was silent in the arena style training yard as everyone watched. Both were standing haphazardly on their feet but they weren't giving up. She swiped his feet out from under him but he twisted yanking her down as well. She kicked his stomach hard and got back to her feet nearly falling again as her balance rocked and vision blurred. He charged at her just as the yell raised of time. He couldn't stop and she was too slow to dodge, they both tumbled to the ground breathing fast.

"Lieutenant Barca, please see the healers, we will notify you of the results."

"Yes sir," Saber still lying on the ground saluted the sky, exhausted. The man she had just fought struggled to his feet and looked her over.

"For a tyke you sure are a wily one," he murmured offering her a hand.

"Your punches are like cannons, I think I want to be like you when I grow up," she mumbled feeling like her brain had been rattled. He roared with laughter and patted her shoulder.

"You should teach me some of those moves you used, I've never seen them before," he told her as he guided her to the healers, "Let's go see Pete, he'll fix us up good as new."

"I think you broke my ribs," Saber winced.

"Is that a complaint from the fearless Saber tooth tiger I've heard so much about?" he glanced back at her.

"No it's a statement, and what's this Saber tooth Tiger bit?" Saber frowned confused.

"It's your nickname the Admiral and Hank's crews call you. You snap when you get angry and attack as if there is no set standards. You were using moves I've never even seen when you let loose. I thought you were in top gear at the start but I was wrong."

"I don't like fighting all out, I like to conserve energy, the Quartermaster and James were both hard fights too."

"True," he nodded, "I watched those too. You did good, kid."

"Thanks," she mumbled as they stepped into Pete's office and were healed completely. Oliver told him to make sure there were no broken bones or injuries and he did just that. Saber sighed feeling better but tired since Pete made your body heal faster as well.

She went out and found Hank standing there with a piece of paper, "You didn't see the HQ General watching did you?"

"No sir," she shook her head, having been completely healed before the other guy she stood exhausted.

"He stated if you didn't want on my ship, he'd assign you directly to HQ," Hank shook his head, "Great fighting out there, Saber."

"I stay with your crew right?"

"Yeah, here are your orders," he nodded.

"Awesome," she mumbled and went to step again only to feel herself falling into blackness. Saber was out although Mason and Hank both rushed to catch her before she fell on her face.

"Man it took three monsters to tire her out," Mason said quietly, "The top fighters in the navy at that."

"True," Hank agreed.

Chapter 4

Six years passed, Saber at 24 was a living legend. She knew a lot about the islands and kingdoms to the point that she was well known as an info broker for the navy. Many captains sought her out before a mission if it was dangerous and many merchants sought her out to find out about the market if they wanted to sell in a new location. She learned the seedy side of life on every island just as well as the political side.

They had not been back to Zosha although Saber talked to the merchants who traveled there to know what they heard. She had her own system of information; she knew information was the key to survival growing up and her curiosity was never satisfied.

They came into HQ Port to report in, Captain Hank knew that Saber was given missions by the Naval General and didn't ask too many questions when she said she needed to do something. It was a new division of the navy called Intelligence or the S-division and he didn't want to deal with that headache so let Saber handle it for him although he and Mason were the only two of the crew to know she was part of that.

Saber frowned leaning on the railing of the stern deck with Hank watching as the crew got them into port. Mason was steering them along easily as always, "I haven't seen her before. Wonder who's visiting our port this time."

"Hard telling," Hank muttered looking at the large ship on dock 3.

Saber stayed on the ship for a while making sure everything was cleaned and ready to go, helping Mason to make sure they both got time away from the ship since they were rarely in port for more than two days. The Naval HQ guards watched their docks so no one had to stay on ship when they were home.

Mason told her to go ahead, there was only two more things and the guys were nearly done. She nodded and stretched up, her sword had broken in the last fight with pirates so she needed to get a replacement. Mason knew she hated going without since they didn't have any extras since six other swords needed replaced for whatever reason. Saber glanced at the Wanted Board before leaving the docks for HQ. She froze seeing Dom and Axel's faces with a high bounty each. Ethan was on there as well having been traveling to the other kingdoms on Zosha's continent. Saber had to walk through the market to get to the HQ buildings and recognized Red shopping for food.

She swung an arm around his shoulders, "To what do I owe the pleasure of seeing your cheerful face in my port, Red?"

"S-Saber?" he looked stunned.

"Walk with me," Saber let him pay before leading him toward the seedier part of town although there weren't any pirates it was just rough crews hanging out there, some merchants hired the more dangerous men to protect from pirates since they weren't always guaranteed a naval escort. Saber stopped at a vendor and bought spices, handing them to Red without saying a word since so many were around.

"Is that the Saber tooth Tiger?" whispers along the street as they walked made Red glance around.

"Is that a nickname for you, Saber?" he asked quietly.

"Is Dom and Axel with you, Red?" she turned to meet his gaze, they were in a quiet stretch of town finally.

"Of course, we are a crew after all," Red nodded.

"Get them and leave as soon as humanly possible," Saber grit her teeth, "Every dock has a wanted board and you are in the Naval HQ Port, there's more navy here than anywhere else. What were you thinking?"

"Well we came to see you," Red watched her, "We've been in town for three days since we heard rumors that you were on your way here."

"Your ship is on the third dock, the galleon I didn't recognize?"

"That's her, we all worked hard to get her," Red grinned, "Isn't she nice?"

"Red, focus, where are those two numbskulls?"

"Said something about trying a restaurant in the market."

Saber turned and walked away, she found them sitting out in the open as if nothing were wrong. She watched a patrol pass them without a glance. She slammed into a seat at their table and glared at them both. Red took the other seat and flushed, "Found her, Cap'n."

"Long time, Saber," Axel greeted.

"I'd say it's great to see you but do you realize who's wanted posters I just saw when I got here an hour ago?" she glared at him, "This is our home port, so eat and get back on your ship or at least try to cover your faces."

"We didn't cruise in with a black flag or anything," Dom shrugged, "They haven't noticed yet."

"Red said you were looking for me," Saber looked at Axel, "I'm going to HQ to report in, I need to hurry before Mason beats me there. Once I report from our last mission, I am going to see your new boat and Red is fixing me one of my favorites since you gave me an ulcer. I want home cooking and I want to see if Red can make the best as a thanks for not arresting us."

She stood and as the waiter came over to the table, "Combatant Commander Barca how are you today, Ma'am?"

"I'm great, take good care of my friends Tommy and put it on my tab," Saber moved away from their table and Axel watched her put her hair into the bun of a naval officer female. She hadn't changed much. They ate quickly and went back to the ship since Red had to cook for her.

Saber went to HQ and tossed her old swords and accepted two brand new ones with black sheathes. The smithy in charge of the swords told her they were made with stronger metals and to test them out for him. If they worked well enough for her then they'd get more of the metal since they always struggled with crap swords.

"Will do," she agreed and reported in, finding Mason just walking in.

"I thought you would be done by now," Mason said surprised.

"Talked swords, Sean wants me to test out these two new swords. If they work well then maybe we won't have trouble with swords snapping."

Saber reported in and Mason invited her to go out to eat but she shook her head, "I ran into a friend in the market, I'm eating with them for supper then home since we are leaving in two days. Auntie and the Old Man said I'm busier than they expected."

She walked out with him and went back to the armory and accepted two of the normal swords just in case. She had four swords but she went to the S-division of HQ and reported there. Spying was what she did all over the known world, she had a huge network and the General knew that. She handed over her coded reports and was about to leave when the S-Division Commander stepped in, "Saber welcome back."

"Sir," she saluted.

"At ease, one of your contacts sent this to us about four days ago. What do you make of it?"

Saber looked over the letter and read the message, there were random capitalized letters and she read the code left there. Saber frowned, "Where did this come from, Zosha?"

"Yep," he agreed.

"I just so happened to see some friends who were recently there, maybe I can get more details."

"If it's true we will have to report it to the king and he might want to discuss this further."

"We will cross that bridge when it comes. I will let you know what I find out," Saber agreed.

She finished reporting and went to the docks. She wasn't in her uniform so many didn't notice although they did notice she was packing four swords, two at her waist and two over her shoulders. She stepped onto the plank leading to the ship and called, "Permission to come aboard?"

"Granted," Anthony grinned watching her with three others staring a hole through her.

"Dang, Anthony you grew!"

"So did you!" Anthony laughed looking her over.

"Hey! I can still kick your scrawny butt, don't be perverted with me."

"Saber," Axel called from the stern, sitting at a table with Dom.

"Red cooking me food?" Saber asked him.

"Yeah," Axel kicked out a chair, "Sit, we need to talk."

"Yes we do," she agreed.

Axel raised an eyebrow and said, "You first."

"Rumor mill says that Zosha is planning to explore the unknown world," Saber met his gaze, "Sending ships around their continent and out to see what they find."

"That is true," Axel nodded, "If people can map the entire world without falling off the edges the king will pay handsomely. Instead of fighting with the explorers who plan to start at Zosha, we decided to come here first to see what you had as far as maps and if you had ever heard what's off the maps beyond this continent."

"Why me?" Saber asked curiously.

"About three years ago we were all surprised to hear your name as an info broker for Ruld," Dom murmured, "We knew you could fight and you were curious about Zosha when you were visiting but we never expected you to be considered an info broker."

"What can I say, I have a curiosity problem," she smiled, "That being said...For this continent we are hemmed in by Lidsing on two of the three borders. Because we are at war with them we don't visit and I have zero contacts to get access to their maps. We have old maps in HQ but it didn't map the entire continent. I'm very interested in it though. I know there are rumors that the continent is a desert the further you go inland and no one can survive so no one explores."

"Bandit's Delight for the lady," Red served a large bowl to Saber and was surprised she grinned excited.

She took a bite and groaned, slapping Dom's hand away from the meal, "Touch and die, Dom."

Dom grinned as Saber looked up at Red, "Is there any way I can steal you away from Axel? Eldridge is good but nowhere near your level, Red."

"That good huh?" Axel chuckled.

"I haven't had this since...three years ago and it wasn't this good because I didn't have all the spices," she sighed, "How long are you staying in port?"

"We were just hanging out to see you," Axel shook his head.

"Give me at least a day, I may have more information," Saber told him, "Red if I buy the ingredients will you make me lunch tomorrow?"

"Just propose to him and join our crew, Saber," Dom laughed.

Saber looked at Dom and said, "Women are different than men it seems because the way to a woman's heart is not her stomach although it earns you points."

Dom laughed as Red flushed. Red murmured, "If you give me enough to cook for everyone we can do that."

"Good," she smiled and hit Axel's hand without even looking back at him, "Axel you know better. If I threaten Dom it stands that I'll threaten you too."

"My ship, my rules, I get to taste anything that comes out of the kitchen," Axel shook his head.

"Then Red can visit my foster family and cook there," she raised an eyebrow, "If he doesn't fall in love with the kitchen I'll eat my swords."

Axel took a small piece and tasted it, "It tastes different from last time, Red."

"I got the right spices, Saber showed me to the vendors who have the good spices earlier."

"The ones on main street don't mix them right, they dilute the blend with salt," she told Red.

She ignored the anger of the crew that heard her threaten their captain, she didn't mind it since she had her food and was eating it happily. She leaned back when she finished and smiled for the first time it felt like in ages. Dom grinned seeing she was relaxed and not angry like she was earlier.

"So you were only angry because we had wanted posters up?" Dom asked her seriously.

"Who did you tick off to earn a wanted poster anyway?" Saber shrugged ignoring the question.

"A nobleman on a fancy ship crossed our path, we didn't kill them but we liberated all their money," Dom told her.

"At least wear hats or something so some wet behind the ears recruits don't recognize you," Saber stretched and yawned, Red took her plate and left quietly, "You have paper on you?"

"Samuel," Axel turned slightly and Samuel went into the captain's quarters to get paper and pen for her. She wrote three recipes and slide them to the side to dry, Dom looked them over and frowned confused.

She sucked at drawing in the first place and she warned Axel it wasn't great but enough to get her point across. She did as much of the coastline as she could remember off the top of her head. "I told you Lidsing has two of our borders. The third is Ilz, a queendom that stays to themselves for the most part. They have a strong army and we have peace with them due to the fight with Lidsing. The coast is mainly cliffs but there are ports, they just have docks at the base of the cliffs and stairs up the side of the cliff. Mostly they have fish markets and nothing else because no one goes to visit. They have traps along the stairs if pirates try to attack that send whoever is trying to come up straight down on the rocks below. Merchants don't visit to sell wares because it's so hard to pack everything up the stairs they just give up and hire a wagon to take them there if they really see profits. I've only been to Isan and Tolan once a piece, sleepy little towns with nothing going on. Past that I've never been and there was no maps or information in the towns to learn what was further along."

"What about the other way?" Dom asked seeing that she stopped halfway across the paper, "Lidsing, what do you know about it?"

"That I went out once that way when there was an attack on our fleet near the border of our waters. We went further than our land and I saw just one port, I don't know the name of it or anything about them. If you want to know about inland where I grew up I could tell you about those villages no problem but not the coast."

"Good to know," Axel murmured.

"I'll check the naval library and the Old Man's library for maps and see if I can't get my hands on maps for you," Saber muttered.

"Why would you do that?" a man with facial hair stared her down, he wasn't angry just curious to who she was. She glanced at Axel and asked, "New friend?"

"Well considering he's been with us for what three or four years now?" Dom looked him over, "Saber this is Gunther—we call him Gun."

"Gun this is Saber, she's a friend we met about six years back," Axel murmured, "She taught us a lot while she visited Zosha."

"Taught what? How to cook?" Gun asked curiously.

"Hey," Red heard that from below, "Don't knock it until you try it!"

"A little of this and a little that," she wasn't too sure about him, "I have my uses."

"Saber, is it true your nickname is Saber tooth Tiger now?" Anthony asked from the lower deck.

"Where'd you hear that?" Saber frowned the faint smile gone, going from friend to naval commander in an instant.

"Red told me," Anthony grinned, "Can I have a round? I want to see if I've gotten any better!"

"She just ate, let her be," Dom growled.

"Just hand to hand!" Anthony pleaded as though he was still a teenager.

"Boy in six years he got chatty," Saber mumbled surprised.

"Hormones," Axel muttered, "Only around pretty ladies does his tongue wag so much."

"I need to head home soon or the old man will send a search party since I'm sure they were told we landed already," she stood with a stretch pulling her swords off and setting them next to the plank and looking at Red, "Watch my stuff."

"Of course," he nodded.

Anthony grinned as she stepped to the middle of the deck and Dom stood moving to the railing, Saber was surprised how many were on the ship, it looked like training on her own which had 200 men, it was close to the same number on their ship. Axel murmured, "Ten minutes, Samuel you keep time."

"Be prepared, I won't hold back since you are an adult and can take care of yourself now, Anthony," Saber warned him.

"All out," Anthony nodded.

She heard Dom's booming voice call start and she attacked first. She swiped his legs out from under him, and before she could follow through he grabbed her legs and yanked pulling her down as well. She got up and got him in a headlock, wrapping her legs around him to hang on. He grabbed the pressure point she taught him and did something she hadn't taught him, reaching for her over his head with one hand he unlocked her legs and yanked her to the ground.

"That's a first," she winced rolling to the side before he followed up on his advantage. She deflected a few fists with barely moving to do so and surprised him with stepping into his defense and using both hands to launch him backward into a crowd of his crewmates. She smiled, "That was a lot nicer than what you did to me although you have learned more since the few weeks we spent together."

"That means a lot," he grinned come back to her, she had launched him so she could fix her shirt, tucking it in so it wouldn't ride up again. She shocked them all when she grabbed his arm and launched herself in the air, wrapping her legs around his neck, pulling them both off balance just as Samuel yelled time.

She let Anthony up and rolled legs over her head into a handstand and back to her feet easily, "Well done, Anthony, I'm impressed."

"What the hell was that at the end?" Samuel asked her, "I've never seen that before!"

"Oh that?" Saber glanced to Samuel as she stepped toward Anthony checking the back of his head, knowing he hadn't been prepared for it before patting his shoulder and turning away, "I meet all kinds of people and learn all kinds of things. That's just a technique I picked up on an island on the edge of the known world."

"Do you mind, Saber?" Dom grinned holding wooden swords. She sighed, "Five minutes and then I'm leaving, I got a lot to do before I can relax and I just got home too."

"Samuel," Axel nodded to him. Saber easily kept up with Dom but he could tell she was holding back.

"Come on, I can tell you are holding back, where's that fighting style that brought your nickname Saber tooth Tiger into the mix," Dom frowned.

"I don't want to show you up in front of the crew or anything," she flashed a grin but it fell instantly, "To be honest I don't like going all out in training, I have three hours of training tomorrow and I won't even have Red's cooking to tide me over in the morning."

"Three hours?" Anthony asked shocked.

"I train with HQ, then with the crew, then while we are in port I'm asked to train other members who have some aptitude for fighting, an hour each."

"Last minute," Samuel called and Saber sighed mumbling that she'd give him a sneak peak and unleashed attack after attack. Dom kept up but only barely and he took surprise kicks to the ribs as well.

Samuel called time and Saber stretched swiping her face with her shirt, uncaring that her tattoo's edge showed or that those in front of her saw she was ripped. She handed Dom the swords back and grinned, "So sensei did I pass your test?"

"Flying colors my pupil," he said formally making her laugh.

"Well I will see you for lunch, and Red I will send ingredients if you are sure you don't want to come to my house and cook for my family," she smiled seeing Red flushed with pleasure.

"Better not, you said your father was an Army hero right?" he shook his head, "I don't want arrested."

"He wouldn't arrest you, he retired last year and him and Giselle enjoy the quiet life...although he does consult for the Navy every once in a while."

"No thanks," Red shook his head.

"Axel has more recipes for you," she put her swords back on and looked up at Axel, "We'll talk business tomorrow at lunch. Don't get arrested, I won't bail you out."

Axel smirked, "One more question, Saber, what's up with the swords, are you learning how to fight with four swords now?"

"Hm?" she cocked her head and then realized she was packing four swords, "Oh! No, the armorer said to test these two out, if they snap I have replacements. One sword snapped in my last fight so I had to replace them. Anyway, see you tomorrow," she went down to the dock and heard a loud greeting from the beach. She ignored all the eyes tracking her as she made it to the wharf, Lincoln was walking with some of his friends who were in the navy. They were in their uniforms although Linc wasn't. Saber knew she was seen as part of the top brass because of her fighting skills, she greeted them and asked what they were doing.

"Walking the wharf to go to the far side of the market for drinks," Linc explained.

"Could you stop these to my room on the ship?" she asked motioning to the two swords over her shoulder. He agreed and took it from her. "Thanks Linc. See you tomorrow."

"Yes ma'am," he nodded, the others saluted her but she quickly saluted back so they weren't drawing attention. She tossed her hair up and jogged toward HQ. She spent an hour in the library copying maps before she went home. She had updated her S-Division commander and he frowned in surprise.

She ate dinner with her family, Ulric and Giselle were happy she was home and asked how everything was going. She told stories on her crewmates and laughed about how the nickname was spreading. Ulric shook his head, "Who would have guessed you'd be a Combatant Commander at the age of 22, you made Ruld history."

"Bandit to Commander, it's crazy right?" she smirked and he shook his head.

"You surprised me," Ulric smirked.

"I ran into some friends, I tried to talk Red into coming to cook for us but he said he wasn't sure he was ready to meet a hero," Saber laughed telling them about Red and how she met him six years ago. She didn't say he was a pirate, only that he was cooking for a ship in port that looked like a large merchant.

"If he makes that pie recipe you gave to Esmerelda ask for a slice to bring home," Giselle smiled. She had been ill for the last two years and the doctors said she wasn't getting enough vitamins so they tried to get the best quality ingredients.

"I'll tell him to make extra," Saber smiled, "I need to go to bed, I have three hours of training tomorrow and I have lunch with them. There is a rumor moving around so I might be leaving again soon."

"That sounds ominous, is everything okay?" Ulric frowned.

"Should be," Saber shrugged, "Who knows until orders come in. Night, love you guys."

Saber hugged them both and kissed Giselle's cheek before going to bed. Her swords next to the nightstand. She woke before dawn and ordered a lot of food to be delivered to Axel's ship and gave a letter to the merchant, "Make sure it gets there before 10am."

"Yes ma'am, but...this isn't your ship."

"No, I am meeting a friend," she smiled, "He's cooking all this for their crew and me."

The merchant smiled surprised, "In that case I will make sure to add the good spices if you are eating it!"

"I wouldn't expect any less," Saber grinned going to training. She took a shower there and changed into her civilian clothes before heading to Axel's ship. She stopped at the top of the plank seeing training going on. She reached over and touched one guy's shoulder and asked where Axel was. He told her to come aboard and he'd take her to him. She had a satchel with her weapons, the crewman didn't say a word just escorted her to them since they all knew her by sight now.

Axel was sitting with four others, Dom one of them, and having a serious conversation. She stopped out of earshot, turning to look at the training on the deck with wooden swords and knives, some hand to hand in one area. It was quiet with tapping of wood against wood the only thing you heard.

"Saber, join us," Axel frowned, "You are early."

"I whipped my guys into shape quickly this morning. Did you get a delivery for Red?"

"It was nearly triple the amount needed for a single meal," Axel nodded, "I think Red was in love at first sight with the spices."

Saber chuckled, "If I'm interrupting a meeting I can come back later."

"No, please sit," Dom murmured getting her chair. She sat and pulled her bag around.

Axel studied her seeing she had dark shadows under her eyes and everyone frowned as she pulled rolls of parchment out of her bag. "I searched the family libraries since the Old Man was an army guy he fought Lidsing and even entered their kingdom a few times. I also searched headquarter libraries this morning and last night. I copied as best as I could all the maps."

She opened the first map and Axel had Dom call the helmsman from training. The four that had been meeting were officers but they were taking turns training below it seemed. "Hunter, pull up a chair."

The man looked about the same age as the rest of the crew, all of them were younger than 25, and this one was blond haired and blue eyes. He sat and looked at the map she had lying open. "Whoa, where'd you get this, Cap'n?"

"Saber will explain it to you," Axel told him watching her.

Saber took time to explain the markings since Ruld coded their maps differently than anywhere else—at least their navy did. "If anyone asks you where you got it, you say it was in your family for generations. I wasn't here and I never gave you anything, understand?"

"Uh, sure," he shrugged.

Red came up with food and Saber told Hunter to roll that one up, they'd look at maps after food. Axel and Dom shared a smirk, Saber really liked

Red's cooking. Saber caught Red's arm and met his gaze, "You said you enhance ingredients right?"

"Yeah," Red frowned confused still balancing a tray. She hesitated but let him go with a slight shake of her head not willing to ask after he slaved over a stove for her. "I saved a pie for you to take home like you asked."

"Thanks," she looked down at the food, "It looks amazing, Red."

"What's wrong?" Red asked as he set the rest of the food down, his helpers assigned to serve the food was already feeding the rest of the crew.

"It's nothing, I just was thinking but it's fine," she shook her head.

Red shrugged getting called away, Saber ate the food she grew up on, she never had time to prepare this meal and she was fighting tears thinking of the neighbor who made it for them all the time. Her brothers fighting for seconds and their father telling them to stop fighting there was plenty. She caught Axel and Dom both studying her in surprise. She shook her head with a grin, "I haven't had this since I was a child. Red is worth his weight in gold, if he wanted to cook for me all the time I'd break the world to make it happen."

Dom laughed, "We wouldn't let him go that easily. You'd have to join our crew before that happened."

"I couldn't do that, it'd break Auntie's heart," she shook her head.

"Who is Auntie?" Hunter asked confused. He hadn't been around when she trained with them. Lagoon who was sitting there with Pierce both told him not to ask questions or he'd regret it. Aware that her family was adopted since her real family was wiped out. Saber smirked at the two, they were always protective of their friends and she liked that about them.

"Giselle Thompson, she and Ulric Thompson took me in when I was 13, I was caught picking pockets and she taught me to read and write. Ulric— the Old Man—always nagged about getting in fights and staying out of trouble. I was a hellion growing up but they are family and it would really upset them if I went back to that way of life. I have a crew who are just as wild and reckless as me which made them really concerned but they've come around."

"They sound awesome," Hunter nodded.

They finished the food and enjoyed the pie, Saber shocked them when Red came back to take their plates and she hugged him tight for a second on tip toe to whisper in his ear that she really appreciated it, she honestly thought those recipes would be lost forever since she never had time or patience to try to make them. Red hugged her tight and thanked her for the recipes. She let go of him and swiped her eyes before turning back to the table and pulled the next map out as if nothing happened.

Hunter asked questions of what she knew about it, surprised she would turn quiet as she thought through what she read. Hunter put the maps away and thanked her for them. Before they went on, a small bell dinged incessantly, Saber pulled a small short wave communications device out, "Combatant Commander Barca."

"Saber we have a Code 3, are you near the ship? We are leaving in ten to assist Admiral Oliver."

"I'm on the wharf, be there in five, any stragglers?"

"Lincoln is rounding them up," Mason told her.

"How many?" Saber growled.

"Fifteen."

"Port announcement, it will take too long to grab them all."

"Captain just ordered that. Code 3 is four to two," Mason reported as Saber grabbed a paper from her bag and wrote her address on it.

"Understood, any others assisting?"

"No ma'am," Mason sounded irritated.

"Any escorts?" she frowned.

"No."

"Be there in a few, over and out."

She looked to Axel, "Can you ask Red to deliver the pie for me? Giselle hasn't been feeling well and was looking forward to it. I won't be back before you leave, I can almost guarantee it. I had more to discuss but it's fine."

"We aren't leaving for another two days, we had some repairs to finish up," Axel shook his head, "Red will deliver it."

"Thanks," she turned and ran to the plank, everyone moved out of her way as she ran. They watched her race to the next dock and onto a ship and make orders as the port echoed a bell style dinging. Saber's voice echoed through the port, "Ship 2 crew, report to duty. Code 3, moving out in five minutes."

She repeated it, and everyone that knew Saber heard the threat in her voice, if they did a port wide announcement and they didn't arrive in time they were disciplined by her and it wasn't fun. Axel looked at the wharf to see people running as fast as possible and civilians moving out of the way. Their crew were not in uniform and from his place on their ship, he could see Saber on the prow helping Mason get them out of their mooring and back into the bay. They took off quickly as Saber yelled for a weapons check.

Axel wondered what a code three was but put it out of his mind as he had Dom summon Red. Dom, Red, and Axel went to the address that Saber wrote. It was a nobleman's house, they could tell instantly as they went to the side door. A woman in the kitchen answered wiping her hands on her apron with a frown.

"Who are you?"

"Sorry ma'am, we are friends of Saber, we were having lunch when she was called away for some kind of code," Axel murmured, "She was excited that Red here made an extra pie for her to take home."

"You must be her friends from Zosha," a tall man appeared behind her.

"Who is at the door, Ulric?" a frail voice came from another room.

"Saber's friends, dear," he announced.

"I'm Axel," Axel introduced.

"I'm Dom," Dom shook his proffered hand, surprised the man didn't seem suspicious at all.

"Come in, we've heard a lot about you from her trip to Zosha, she said Red was an amazing cook. Have you already had desert?"

"Yes sir," Axel flashed a smile.

They went to the dining room as the cook got plates and forks. Axel looked around in surprise as Giselle coughed into a napkin before saying, "Saber was called away so soon, we were looking forward to spending the afternoon together too."

They ate the pie in shock looking to Red, "This is amazing!"

"Thank you," Red blushed as red as his hair.

Before they left, Red surprised Axel with looking to Ulric who walked them to the front door, "Can I ask what's wrong with Lady Giselle?"

"Doctors say her body isn't getting enough vitamins and nutrients from food. We buy the best ingredients but nothing seems to be working for her. Saber doesn't say much but brings home a lot of different spices and things from other countries to try their medicinal qualities but nothing has worked. She's developed a weak immune system and easily gets sick. Saber wouldn't have said anything about it because that's her, she worries without saying a word."

"I see," Red murmured, "I might have something that could help from Zosha, she hasn't been there in years so maybe she hasn't heard of it."

"We couldn't possibly ask you to do that, you boys have work to do," Ulric shook his head.

"I insist, Saber helped me and I still owe her one," Red told him, "I'll be back tomorrow morning."

"Thank you for the visit, it made our day meeting some of Saber's friends, she doesn't have many that visit. Do me a favor though," Ulric stepped closer to Dom and Axel, "Wear a hat or something in public, you both are wanted after all."

"Uh," Red looked at the two in surprise.

The two looked shocked and Ulric chuckled, "No funny business and I don't care if you visit my daughter but break a law in front of me and that's a different story."

"No sir, we keep our noses clean, it was a misunderstanding that led to those posters," Axel smiled.

"That's what Saber says when she doesn't want in trouble...disarming smile and all," Ulric laughed, "See you boys soon, come back any time. Tell us some stories about Saber, she can't tell us what she does anymore but I'm sure you have some good stories to tell."

"Saber wanted Red to cook for you, she gave him her recipes from home and said she wanted you to try more. We might come back when she is here to have Red do just that."

"Good," Ulric nodded and they left.

Chapter 5

Saber was in the middle of preparing for battle, a Code 3 was a fight with Lidsing navy near the border. Four ships against two of their fleet, Saber didn't like when it was outnumbered like that. The fight was rough and Hank was injured badly to the point he was taken to the doc. When that happened technically Mason would be in charge but because it was a fight Saber got that honor. She protected Mason who was fighting to keep their ship from tangling masts with a Lidsing ship. The sailing crew were struggling to cut the enemy's sail so they were unhooked while also fighting Lidsing sailors who were trying to protect their sail. Mason yelled at one of the archers on deck to aim at the enemies on the mast as he struggled with maneuvering their ship. Saber fought Lidsing navy that landed on the stern but also kept an eye on the deck below.

"John!" she bellowed and a whole squad stopped as John turned to look up at her, fighting to keep enemies away from him as they talked. Saber was fighting still but continued with her order, "Get up here with your squad and keep the stern free of Lidsing!"

"Yes ma'am," he gave orders to his group and they came up just as she dispatched her opponent she had been fighting. Saber stood on the railing and made orders loudly to her crew, they continued to fight but obeyed her orders. Mason bellowed orders to the sailing crew who were working like a well oiled machine. Saber made a quiet order into a tube that led to the cannons, it was a quick communications and they agreed, soon had a sunk enemy ship and those on deck surrendered and were chained in the brig. Saber turned and looked to Mason, a cut on her cheek from an arrow that barely missed her eye, "Next pretty please."

"Yes ma'am," Mason flashed a grin at her overly polite order.

"Prepare starboard attack," Saber ordered as Mason brought them around Oliver's ship and they attacked hard and fast. She looked to the Admiral's ship to see Oliver was bleeding and looked hurt. Saber waited as they cleared the admiral's ship and ordered to fire. Her crew knew to aim as far down as possible to hit the water line, it was Saber's repetition that made them automatically do so. The Lidsing ship took on water and started to sink as they watched the keel shatter. Two down, Saber thought. They fought the last two ships and in middle of the commotion, as things were winding down, Saber looked to Mason, "I'll be back, stay as close as possible to this ship."

He frowned but watched her jump to the Lidsing ship, the crew had abandoned the ship and were swimming toward shore nearly two miles away, she searched for maps and information. She grabbed all of it as she felt the ship yawn to one side. She came out and jumped to their deck. She set the stuff in her room and back to the stern looking to Mason as she said, "I officially give you command, sir."

"Don't freak me out," Mason glared but knew she was doing something that would benefit them later. She flashed a smile and he knew she couldn't promise that. They limped back to HQ, towing the Admiral's ship. Saber made orders as Mason did his helmsman duties. She stood on the railing with her arms folded watching everyone and barking orders fast. She had those of the fighting crew cleaning up so that there was less work on the sailing crew when they got into port. She had people running reports and giving her papers as she continued to bark orders. Mason told her they needed to cut the Admiral's ship loose as long boats came out to meet them. She made the order since Mason had been yelling just as much but his voice was shot. Her voice caught but they could hear her clearly as she continued string after string of orders. It took them a full night to get back to port, it was nearly noon as they coasted in.

When they got in she read the reports on strips of papers from the cannon crew, and lower decks. She assigned John's squad and two others to escort the injured to the infirmary since the doctor on ship couldn't keep up with everyone. She looked to Mason, "The brig is full, we need guards to march them to holding in HQ."

"I can take it from here, go check on Oliver and then go to the infirmary for a report of injured and check on our guys. I will be here until you get back."

"Yes sir," she handed him the reports, ducked into her room grabbing her satchel and tossing everything into it haphazardly before taking a rope and jumping to the other ship, landing on the rail and asking permission to board. James nodded and waved her over.

"Need any assistance?"

"Your men alright, I heard you yelling all night so is Hank down?"

"Injured and heading to HQ infirmary. You?"

"Oliver was wounded and I'm in charge. If you would go to HQ and ask for all available hands to help us get these Lidsing to the holding cells and clean up the ship would be great. We are lean on men, most are wounded and exhausted."

"Understood," she took off quickly and made orders loudly for all available personnel to report to the docks. She then went to report directly to the General who wanted an update although all three captains had been seriously wounded and the next in command were trying to finish up getting docked. She explained high level what happened and he understood reports would be written once everyone completed the task of getting into port. He went with her to oversee the captive Lidsing navy members after checking on the injured in the infirmary. The doc there said they were all going to survive but some injuries would leave deep scars and lessen mobility. Saber went back to her ship and gave an update to Mason as captives were frog marched up to the HQ building. Saber hadn't had time to look at what she had stolen but took a moment as Mason made final orders and they were waiting for that to be done. She found complete maps of Lidsing territory which they had never gotten before. She looked at the log book of the ship and found it was in Lidsing, she'd have to translate it later. Mason glanced over her shoulder and raised an eyebrow at all the paperwork she was slowly putting in order.

"Is that good?" he asked.

"It's great," she smiled.

"Well at least we got something more than just captives for our trouble," Mason sighed.

"I need to report to S-Division," she said softly and he nodded, "I'll contact you on the comms if I need anything. Write your report while you are there."

"Of course," she nodded, "I'm going home after that if you need me."

"Sounds good," he nodded.

She went to S-Division and copied the maps, making three—one for Hank and their crew, one for s-division, and one for Axel although she wasn't telling anyone that. The original was staying with her. She could copy another for others later on. She had a feeling Axel would return in kind or she wouldn't have bothered. Her report and everything was done and she went to the wharf where shipwrights were fixing the ships. She went to Dock 3, she had noticed it was still there although she didn't realize how bad she looked as she made it to the top of the plank and met Dom and Axel there. Dried blood like war paint ran from just shy of her eye down her neck.

"Have a minute?" her throat felt raw and croaked on the words. Their crew was silent as they studied her.

"Come back in the morning, go sleep, you look like you had a rough time of it," Dom offered.

"I don't know when we are leaving again, might as well get this info to you now."

"What is it that could be this important?" Axel asked surprised.

"You know you're right, I need a shower," she mumbled, "Meet me at my house. Talk Red into coming to cook, I'm starving and he's within walking distance."

She pouted to Axel who looked surprised, she never acted like that before. Dom chuckled, "You look like you fought a war."

"It wasn't fun," Saber shook her head and glanced down, "Forgot I'm a bloody mess, thanks for the reminder, Giselle would faint if she seen me like this. I think I gotta…"

She pulled her satchel around and rummaged in her kit, she pulled out a cloak and flipped it over her shoulder and around to cover most the blood and flashed a smile, "You'll like my surprise but I need a promise in return. We'll talk once I clean up. Drinks on me tonight, I'm gonna drink 'til I pass out!"

She waved leaving them completely confused at why she was so random. She went into the back door and took a long hot shower. She came out feeling better although her face ached where the arrow got her. She heard voices in the library and went that way. She found Axel and Dom talking with Giselle and Ulric. She froze surprised, "Hey."

"Red is cooking," Dom told her with a grin. She smiled flopping into a seat next to Giselle with a contented sigh.

"Saber?" Giselle was surprised.

"He's the best cook, if he ever marries I'll cry," Saber told her and smiled as Giselle laughed.

"Is someone interested?" Giselle laughed.

"He's a sweetheart but no, not my type. That and I couldn't possibly steal him from Axel and his friends. It would ruin our friendship," Saber sighed. If she had a type she wouldn't admit it to Giselle but a certain pirate captain that was quiet and studying her would be right up her alley although she wouldn't ever admit or risk it since he was a wanted man.

"Are you sure you are good, Saber, you are acting weird," Axel frowned watching her.

"She only gets this way after a long fight and over exhaustion," Ulric explained, "Come to the dining room."

They walked to the dining room as Giselle laughed at Saber who yawned. Red was placing food on the table when they walked in, "Lucky for you I was already here cooking when you stopped by the ship. Lady Giselle invited me to steal the kitchen. They have some guests coming."

"Guests?" Saber froze looking to Giselle.

"Sorry Saber, we expected you to be gone another night," Ulric murmured.

"He's a respectable young man, his mother is a dear friend of mine," Giselle pouted, "Ulric you know if Saber was raised in Court she'd—"

"But she wasn't," Ulric started.

"Auntie," Saber complained.

"Just for an hour, you can last that long," Ulric sighed watching Saber.

Saber slammed into a chair and crossed her arms, "If they take much longer I'm eating and running for the hills."

"Lady Giselle your guests have arrived," the steward announced speaking over her mutter.

"Hello Lady Amber, Lord Ruben, and Lord Justin," Giselle greeted. They came in and sat with them, everyone was quiet as they sat together. Red served every course; Saber noticed the dessert was her family recipe. She didn't talk about work, only excused herself for the evening. Of course, Axel and Dom excused themselves soon after and met her in the kitchen. Justin seemed interested in her but she didn't give any hint that she wanted pursued, shutting down every advance like a tactician in battle to the point Axel and Dom felt a little sorry for him. Saber was sitting waiting with Red in the kitchen when they came around the house, "Let's go!"

They followed her to the seedy part of town, she waved her hand at the bar maid as she sat at a table with one man, "Scat."

"Who're you?" he growled.

A man behind him whispered in his ear and he nearly fell standing fast and moving away. They had three large pitchers of ale in front of them fast, the barmaid murmured, "Joseph said to find him if I found you before he did."

"I'll see him tomorrow. Keep the ale coming."

"Yes ma'am," she smiled.

Red didn't drink much, the others kept up with her but nearly failed since she planned to be blasted drunk by the end. Axel leaned forward, "Before you get too drunk tell us what you stopped by the ship this afternoon about."

"I'll explain it to Hunter at dawn, keep it safe, and it's been in your family for ages," she smirked passing the map under the table.

"What do I have to promise in keeping this?" Axel was serious.

"If you travel you bring me a map in return of everywhere you go," her eyes danced.

"That's easy enough," Axel smirked.

They drank until Saber was singing bandit shanties she grew up on to everyone's shock and amusement. Axel looked at the guys and looked at the barmaid, "Can I get the check please?"

"It's taken care of, Saber pays ahead so she doesn't have to remember. She only brings a friend or two that will make sure she gets home safely so be sure to make that happen or the whole port city will have your heads, she's our beloved warrior girl."

"Of course," Axel agreed.

Saber was singing another one as Red and Dom helped her stand to her feet. She complained that they weren't singing with her, she switched to a sea shanty that they knew and they joined in as they walked. When Axel led them toward her house, she stumbled into Axel's chest when he turned toward her to warn her to quiet down since they were nearly there. She giggled resting her forehead against his chest for a second, "I can't keep my balance even with Red and Dom to hold me up."

He scoffed softly shaking his head, "Nearly there, Saber."

She let him push her off his chest, and yawned feeling the exhaustion from the last few days hit. They went to the back of the houses and to the kitchen door. She caught Axel's hand shocked he was going to knock. She pointed to the top of the door and he frowned confused. "Loose stone, there's a key just for me."

Axel shook his head shocked that she was telling him where to find a key. They unlocked the door and Axel took her, telling the other two to wait for him at the gate. He helped her up to her room and asked if she was fine. She agreed and met his gaze, "Thanks, Axel."

"See you at dawn," Axel whispered.

"Lock the door when you leave, please," she fell back on the bed, eyes closed in sleep before he even left the room. He paused at the door to look back only to find her turn and curl into a ball on the bed. He shut her door and slipped down the back hallway to the back door which he locked and slipped the key back into it's hiding place before out again to the gate. She woke just before dawn smelling coffee.

Esmerelda smiled as Saber followed her nose out the door, "That smells amazing."

"Red left a lot of different ingredients and said he loved on them. He gave a special tea to Giselle as well, it's a huge bag."

"He enhances ingredients to the best possible degree," Saber rubbed her forehead, "Thanks for the coffee. Did I wake anyone when I came in?"

"No we were surprised to find you home at all, normally when you go out with friends you make some kind of ruckus when you come back," Esmerelda laughed softly.

"It was needed, they must have helped me in last night," Saber rubbed her forehead as she sipped the coffee. Her hangover was horrible but it was manageable. She changed and went out the back, hoping to catch Red cooking again. She arrived at Dock 3 to find everyone eating breakfast, "Room for one more?"

"Get up here, your food is about to get cold," Axel summoned her up. She sat and smiled seeing the map she had copied on the table as they ate.

"Where'd you get such a detailed map?" Hunter asked as she ate.

"The Code 3," she shook her head, "We...well let's just say I had fun and I have a bad habit of fighting dirty. The ship was about to sink and I...liberated the map along with other things since the people jumped ship."

"Pirates?" Dom frowned, "A map this good?"

"No worse than pirates," she grumbled.

"What's considered worse than pirates to a navy girl like you?" Lagoon frowned.

"Doesn't matter," Saber shook her head, "Anyway you have a map, the navy has a copy now, and I have a copy. Yours is a family inheritance and I never want you to ask for the story again. It was the worst day and I drank it nearly into oblivion."

"Was Oliver and Hank alright," Axel asked seriously.

"Axel," she warned, her eyes ice cold compared to the sky blue they were used to. She was a cold blooded commander who warned to stay on her good side. Axel raised his hands and was saved by the comms unit in her pocket dinging.

"Barca," she growled still ticked off.

"Report to HQ, General wants to see you immediately," the Quartermaster ordered.

"Did he give a reason?" Saber winced.

"You might want to dress in uniform, over and out."

She cursed standing and looking at Axel, "You will be here when I'm done, right? I had more to discuss before you disappear into unknown waters for who knows how long."

"I'll be here until dawn tomorrow," Axel studied her, she turned to leave and glanced back at him.

"Thanks for yesterday, I don't relax with just anyone around," she met his gaze, "I needed it."

"Go before I have a General coming to find you on my ship," Axel smirked.

Saber smirked jogging to her ship. They noticed her walking briskly down the wharf in her uniform looking beautiful. "The ice princess," Dom murmured watching Axel as everyone saw Saber leave.

"Ice Princess?" Axel cocked his head.

"She doesn't show it often but she is dangerous when she gets angry and reminds me of a cold blooded killer about to strike," Dom agreed.

"True," Pierce murmured, "The fight with bandits, she mercilessly slaughtered all of them even when they begged her to not kill them."

"It's a nicer nickname than Saber tooth Tiger," Red muttered, "Wonder what she has to do now."

Two hours later they heard the port wide announcement, "Attention all, Navy HQ will announce awards to key individuals who showed valor and strength in combat two days ago against Lidsing navy ships attacking our waters. Please help us celebrate their accomplishments."

Names were announced until it got to officers, they were being awarded rank promotions and other such things. Saber was not promoted but awarded a medal of valor and a Star of Excellence. "This is her second star of Excellence, she has broken Ruld history being the first to receive two stars under the age of 45. Other awards have been given for battle tactics. Captain Hank Jones is elevated to Vice Admiral."

Oliver got an award as well but Axel had zoned out. They went to the market, wearing hats since Saber would yell if they didn't. Saber, Mason and four others of their crew were trying to get out of the market area and to the houses beyond but everyone who saw them had to stop and congratulate them. Saber was frowning but Mason looked pale.

Axel saw the two stars pinned to her chest with other pins showing her rank and accomplishments. A lot larger pile than the others she was walking with, he noticed. Saber finally took point of their group and announced for the entire market to hear, "Thank you all for your congratulations but we have work to do. Maybe later we can all celebrate after the work is done."

"Come to my bar, Saber tooth Tiger! Drinks on me for you and your crew."

"We couldn't put you out like that, Mason here would drink the bar dry!" Saber smirked walking on.

Her smile dropped as soon as she passed the barkeep who offered, Axel could tell she wasn't too thrilled but wasn't about to walk up to her with her crew behind her. He heard Mason asking, "Are you sure you want to do that, Saber?"

"I'm going home, Mas," she met his gaze, "You'll know if I do it or not when you see me next time. Make sure the shipwrights get the ship done as soon as possible, we are leaving at dawn."

"Why us?" Lincoln complained as they passed Axel and Dom who were listening hard although facing a vendor so they went unnoticed.

"Because half the crew are former pirates," Mason growled at Lincoln, "If you don't want to come you know the only way out is cutting off a limb, Linc. Orders from the king, suck it up."

"If you cut off a limb I'll kill you," John growled at Linc, "We've put time and energy into training you right. Noble or not, you are part of the crew."

"I don't want to cut off a limb, I'll never hear the end of it from my family if I did that," Lincoln shook his head, "If we don't die I'd say it's good timing since mom's trying to marry me off."

"You too huh?" Saber scoffed.

"What?" the other crew members asked loudly causing everyone to turn to them in shock. She glared at them in warning, "Go home, pack your kits for a long journey and I don't want to hear another word out of you about anything!"

"Ma'am," they saluted, hearing her tone meaning to tread carefully.

She saluted and they raced off toward home. She went home and changed clothes, she left her uniform there and packed her kit. She ate on the back balcony with the family before going to Dock 3. She talked with Anthony while waiting for Axel and the others to come back since they were buying supplies. Mason was taking care of all that for their ship and she made an order in the comms to the armory for extra weapons and cannons, the ship would be stuffed to the gills with food and supplies. Anthony watched her as she sat on their ship making orders of everything she knew they would need. At the very end of her list which Dom and Axel heard as they walked up the plank, "I need kits supplied for five recruits. We are getting wet behind the ears kids on this voyage and I want them to have double of everything—understand? Make sure everyone has at least one replacement weapon and stash whetstones as well."

"How long of a voyage is this?"

"I don't know!" she growled, "Just deliver it to Vice Admiral Hank's ship before dawn. If it's not there before four am I'll be visiting you and you won't like it!"

"Aye-aye ma'am, over and out."

Saber looked up to see who blocked the sun from her face, "I was working while I waited."

"What was that about, you are taking off on another mission?" Axel asked curiously.

"I need to talk to you privately," Saber stood to face him.

Dom frowned and before he could say anything, Axel said, "Dom too."

"Fine, no one else," Saber nodded.

Axel led to his captain's quarters and sat at his table studying Saber who sat with them catching her eyes looking around at the clean interior in surprise. "What's this about, Saber?"

"This is life or death for me, Axel so no one outside of this room can hear or know about it," she met his gaze.

"Okay," Dom agreed as Axel nodded once.

"A few years back the navy caught wind of my nickname of the info-broker. They created an intelligence division, I have contacts all over the known world and if I can't find the answer then no one can—they believe. Except Lidsing anyway. Long story short, I'm the second in command of the Intelligence wing. We heard rumors of Zosha exploring the day before you arrived from a contact there. The map was from Lidsing ships that I gave you last night. The king has been told Zosha wants to map more of the world and he doesn't want left behind since we don't even have our entire continent mapped. If Zosha maps their unknown side and we map ours, we both win without stepping on each other's toes. He doesn't know you are in port and planning to head that way. Since I got the map from Lidsing we've been issued orders to go to Ilz and map that side until we reach the mapped Lidsing side if possible. Once that's complete we are to explore out from there. To help us both out if you go Lidsing and around and we meet at the back of the continent—if there is a back—then we can both explore and knock two birds with one stone."

"It makes sense," Axel frowned, "What if we don't meet you though?"

"Then you are just validating the map you have and you do what you want from there," Saber met his gaze.

"Agreed," Axel nodded, "Works for us. Do you want to shake on it?"

"I want to know who did your tattoo on your arm," she reached out to touch the design lightly.

"Pierce did it, he apprenticed with a tattoo shop in Zosha before he started running with us," Dom chuckled.

"You think he has time to give me one?" Saber asked curiously, "The one tattoo I have is a stamp of my past, I want one I will like that means something to me in the present."

"Sure," Axel smirked, "Get this in the same place as a sign we are friends."

Saber studied him in surprise, "You always surprise me, Axel."

"I hope this bad idea works for us," he looked at the map again, "I can't speak Lid."

"It's easy," Saber switched from Zo which she always spoke with them to Lid with ease.

"Any words would help," Dom agreed, "What did you say?"

"It's easy," Saber translated and taught them words carefully writing them and how to sound them out compared to Zo words. She dug in her satchel, having went home she grabbed her books of the different languages to refresh how she learned before trying Ilz or going to an unknown country. She gave Axel and Dom her book on Lidsing which was written in Common.

"Knowledge is power," Saber smirked.

They went out as Axel tucked the book under his arm, "Pierce get your tattoo kit."

"Aye sir," he frowned confused but obeyed, "Who's getting ink?"

"Saber, make it exactly like mine," Axel murmured opening the book to start reading. Pierce looked at his design again before starting. She sat where he told her and held her arm on the table. Anthony brought rope to tie her wrist down so she wouldn't move too much. Saber relaxed as she watched Pierce set up.

"At least this time I get to watch," she grinned when Dom asked why she looked excited, "Last time my father strapped me down to a bed and whoever's house it was they used an herb to knock me out, when I woke up my back was on fire and hurt like hell."

"Well don't tense," Pierce met her gaze, "Don't move at all if you can help it. Anthony can get you a rag or something so you won't scream if you get too loud."

"I'll be fine," Saber smirked, "Let's go, I still have work here to get done before I leave."

She had taught the intelligence wing how to decipher the messages to her that came in from everywhere. She didn't visit most places often so it wouldn't worry them if she was out of port for years at a time but her contacts in town were a different story. She watched as Pierce started the process, she didn't make a peep just stared fascinated as he swiped blood away and continued.

Axel asked her questions on certain words and she answered, her eyes never leaving the tattoo. When Pierce finished, he told her to see a healer before taking off or put salve on it three times a day until it healed and not to let it be in the sun at all until it was 100% healed. He wrapped it up and she smiled, "I like the design."

"It's a Zosha original, only the original crew with Axel have it and you," Lagoon told her.

"What does it mean exactly other than friend," she met Axel's eyes when they shot up to meet her curious gaze.

"A compass to guide your way and the ship to get you there," he looked at her wrapped arm, "The swords to protect you on your journey and the words mean just what they say."

"Seize the day," she smiled, "Thanks Pierce, hopefully we see each other soon."

"Was that everything you wanted to tell us?" Dom frowned, "You said there was more but I don't think what we talked about was it."

"While I was sitting on my hands, I translated most the log book I found which talks about the voyage the ship took but anything worth mentioning is on the map so it was worthless to grab. Oh Red," Saber caught him about to start a late lunch, he looked up at her surprised, "Thank you for helping Giselle, it means the world to me."

"I hate to bring up the past but we still owe you for six years ago, Saber," Red grinned, "I'm just helping until we can pay it back."

"Alright I have business to finish, you have final stuff to get done, and I am in the way. If we don't see each other in six months we continue as if on our own," Saber met Axel's eyes and he agreed.

"Good luck out there," he nodded.

"If you find any islands or kingdoms outside of Lidsing get books and information," she waved walking away.

She went to see Joseph who had contacts in different islands, Saber told her contacts around town to drop off information to Rebecca at the tavern. She was an intelligence officer in the navy who married the barkeep and worked there to gather information from merchants and navy alike. No one knew she was intelligence although only her crew, the Admiral's ship, knew she was navy, having been reassigned to the Admiral's ship after Saber left.

Chapter 6

Dawn the next day they took off. Hank was still injured but alive. Saber noticed Axel's ship leaving at the same time and waved. Hank frowned, "Who was that?"

"Don't yell," Saber turned to him, "He brought great intel with him since he is one of the explorers. Axel and Dom with a crew of nearly 200."

"He doesn't fly a black flag but I would have sworn there was a wanted poster," Hank smirked as Saber innocently asked if there was, she wasn't sure. Being second in command of the intelligence wing meant she was on top of the information and playing dumb was just a joke.

"Less backtracking if it works, I take it you asked him to go that way and we meet up to share maps for a complete continent before adventuring out to the great unknown?"

"Exactly, if within six months we don't see each other, we pretend we never made the agreement and proceed with the order to map the entire continent before going out away from the continent."

"Good plan, Saber."

"We have five recruits, I checked everything even their kits," Saber informed him.

"Did you sleep at all?" Hank asked rubbing his arm which was healed but still tender, the doctor did a lot for him but he was still healing. Saber had stopped to see a Navy doc who healed her arm without comment at the tattoo. She still had it covered and put salve on it so that it stayed hydrated and healed well.

"A little bit, I heard we had a map maker with us?"

"Yes," Hank nodded, "He's assigned to us from HQ and not exactly happy about it. He will track reefs and shoals as well as other oddities on the map."

"Sweet," Saber was happy she didn't have to do it since it meant that he was trained to draw maps and would make beautiful ones.

"What's up with the arm, you injured or something?"

"Or something," she smiled, "I got a tattoo but didn't want Lady Giselle freaking out on me."

"I see," Hank chuckled, "I hope it's a good one."

"It has meaning so it is," she agreed.

They traveled Ilz without stopping at the two ports they knew about, the third they slowly went past, giving enough time to look at the layout of the stairs and move on. Saber wrote in a new journal about everything in case they needed it. Months passed with nothing going on, the Ilz country was nothing but cliffs, when they came to another village they stopped. A man was at the docks at the bottom of the cliff and asked who they were in common. "Explorers just passing through," Saber answered, "We want to map the entire continent and started in Ruld. We need to refresh our supplies, may we go up?"

"Sure but there isn't a market except for fish," the man growled, "A well in the village can refill your fresh water but it's nearly dry so don't expect more than a barrel."

"Thank you," Saber murmured and they packed an empty barrel up with them. Eldridge bought fish and what little spices they had, it was similar stuff to Ruld so Saber wasn't too impressed yet but she asked around about what to expect as they continued. An old man heard the question and said, "There should be a village about three days sail if the wind is good. The cliffs stay through the desert lands and then slowly come down to the ocean."

"Do you have a map of the coast line?"

"No," they didn't have anything like that, they were just fishermen and the only reason he knew about that village was because a storm came out of nowhere and he was pulled that far away. Saber nodded and went to join with her squad, they were still in Ilz at least. The old man didn't say if the next village was Ilz or not. She turned back to ask and he shrugged, "They spoke common and I didn't ask."

"Thanks again!" she went down the stairs and they continued to sail. The men fished off the sides to continue getting fresh meat and save their salted meat below. As for the vegetables they were getting lean. Saber hoped the next village would have more. When they arrived they found a huge market and she asked where they were. "Ilz of course."

She found maps for sale and bought a map that showed islands out from there. Saber was excited, they had made progress. She handed the map to Killian who held onto it although his maps were to be precise so he couldn't take their word for it, Saber's crew would have to make it to each of those islands before they existed on his map. Saber understood his need to be precise and asked more questions. Pirates were a problem for them and it was considered lawless on this side of the continent as far as the ocean went. Ilz didn't have a navy so they suffered attacks all the time. Saber picked up a book to learn their language and found books on their desert plants and how to find water in the desert. They left, they were close to the Lidsing border from what the villagers in the market said. The weather was getting cold as they moved around the continent.

"Looks like a storm," Hank frowned up at the black clouds ahead of them. It looked as if that was the only cloud in the sky, it was odd the way it looked but a pirate ship appeared in the storm to attack them. Saber fought hard but during the storm, which the pirate captain controlled, Saber fought one of the monstrously strong pirates, she gave him a fatal wound as he charged her and they both went overboard. In the craziness of the situation Mason ordered one of the crew to drop a longboat as a few others were tossed off the ship. Saber got in the longboat with the others and tried to go back to the ship but the wind was against them and they only had one oar. The storm was pushing them away, going further around the coast the way they were headed. They were all injured and exhausted. Saber told them to rest, she watched the coast knowing that Hank would catch up, her head hurt and was bleeding.

The storm seemed to have expanded and they were drenched as they floated along the coast. Two days passed when Saber found another ship appeared. She frowned hoping it was a merchant ship. She waved seeing oars out each side as they fought against the wind toward Saber's long boat. They had drifted with no sign of Hank and had no water or anything.

It was cold, winter in that part of the world and they weren't dressed for it. She heard shouts and rope ladders were tossed over to let them up. Saber tie the longboat to the ladder and went first in case it was a trap. She came over the side and found Dom and Axel there to face her prepared if she were an enemy. She sighed in relief and looked over the side, "All good, come up!"

Axel stepped forward to look her over, "Doc!"

Saber shaking in the freezing cold and exhausted from staying awake, stumbled, and caught herself on the railing as her men came up, all of them shaking in the cold wind. Axel made orders for blankets and something warm to drink if Red could get it in the choppy weather.

The doc treated their injuries, Saber sat huddled near the prow as she finished explaining what happened and they continued forward to see if Hank and Mason were alright. Axel went to stand and she caught his hand, "Thanks Axel. I owe you."

Saber shivered in the chill and was shocked that Axel gave her a cloak with a hood along with the blanket she was already wrapped in. "Rest, Saber."

He could tell she was freezing and worried for the rest of the crew. She must have dozed because she woke to yells of a ship. She stood unsteadily to her feet and looked out, she relaxed seeing it was her ship heading toward them. Axel recognized it and saw Saber's shoulders relax, he made fast orders and they brought a shuttered lantern for Saber to signal them. Saber signaled fast and they anchored together tying the ships together to meet and weather the storm.

Hank greeted Dom and Axel like sons, not caring if they were pirates or what they were, he hadn't seen them in nearly seven years at that point. "Saber said we would run into each other and I was excited to see you."

"We validated the map and added more to it," Axel said calling Hunter, "Hunter and Pierce drew it to make it as close as humanly possible."

"Killian," Hank turned and the map maker stepped forward showing his map. Axel was surprised at how little there was.

"There was a village a little ways back that had everything known to man if you need to restock," Dom told them.

"We just topped everything off three days back at the last village," Mason shook his head, they did a quick stop to see if Saber was there at the village they had seen before moving on, "Thanks though. Saber also found a map of some of the unknown world although probably not all of it."

"So did we, let's compare and plan where we are heading," Axel smirked.

They were in his captain's quarters since it was snowing, Saber still felt like she couldn't get warm and pulled her knees up to her chest as she sat in her chair next to Axel and Mason. Axel noticed she was shivering even with the cloak she wore, it was warm with so many bodies but being on the long boat with no winter gear must have gotten a chill in her bones. He glanced to Dom, "Have Red make soup and tell him put a little extra pizzazz in it."

"Aye," Dom moved to the door and Axel leaned back to reach his bed and grabbed the blanket. Saber didn't try to play like she wasn't freezing, she wrapped it around her as well and ignored the look Killian and Hunter were giving her.

"Thanks, Axel," she mumbled, the hood of the cloak was up and the only thing they could see clearly was her nose.

"Can't have the Saber tooth Tiger frozen like a popsicle on my watch," Axel shrugged, "Alright Hunter walk Killian through what we found and added to the map."

"Sir," Hunter leaned forward to point out everything they added to the map although it was minimal. Their map of islands further out looked different from what Saber found. Killian pointed out one of the islands and murmured, "That looks like it's on both maps although they are slightly different."

"Alright we explore in circles and land on that island. If anything happens, we continue to move. If we don't show up then I'm sure you will map our islands afterward and if you don't show up, we check yours. If we get more maps that have more information on them then we keep going. If not then if nothing bad happens we discuss next steps from there," Axel murmured, "Not that anything will happen."

Saber watched and continued to be quiet as they planned. She fell asleep as they talked late into the night. She was balanced so well on the chair that no one noticed. Axel looked at Hank who tugged her hood back slightly. Saber had fever flushed cheeks and her eyes were closed sleeping soundly. Axel murmured, "Saber how many attackers were on that ship?"

"Estimate 320, over 200 fighters," she mumbled.

Axel raised an eyebrow and Hank nodded slightly that she was right. "Are you asleep?"

Saber didn't respond, she was good at answering when she heard her name but if she were tired she slept through anything. Axel stood and shocked all of them with gently slipping his hands under her knees and around her back, Saber spoke in Ruld but Axel was rusty in understanding. Hank and the navy frowned worried.

"What did she say?" Hunter asked.

"Nothing worth repeating," Mason shook his head, aware she was dreaming of the dead again. Killian didn't know her history but she said father so he assumed she was dreaming of home.

Axel laid her down and made sure the blanket was wrapped around her before sitting down again, "Dom ask the doc to check her again."

"Aye," Dom opened the door to make the order, the doc came and checked her again, aware of all the officers watching him in silence.

"She has a fever but it could be from being out in the cold for too long. We are out of blankets but it's warm enough in here to keep her from worsening. I recommend she stay here until the fever breaks, going into the storm even for a quick walk to the other ship could make it worse since it's a high fever."

"Mason go to her room and get warmer clothes and her blanket off her bed," Hank muttered.

Mason went to do that and came back with folded clothes and her blanket wrapped in a cloak. He set the clothes on Axel's bedside stand and laid the blanket over Axel's own and the cloak over that. They continued discussions, the doc set a water basin and clothe in the room, setting a cool clothe on her forehead. Dom sat beside Axel and switched her clothe as they talked. When everyone left, no one realized it was Axel's bed that Saber was lying on as they went to their own ships and their own beds. Axel sighed having went out to see them off his ship before turning and going back to his room. Saber was still fever flushed and mumbling uncomfortably in her sleep. He changed the wet cloth and pulled the blankets up over her where she had shifted in her sleep. He sat in a chair watching over her for the night. He pulled a hammock from under the bed and strung it up, sometimes it was too much to sleep on a stable bed at sea so he'd sleep in the hammock. He switched her clothe again before lying down. He got up when she started mumbling to reapply the cool clothe but otherwise slept.

Dom tapped and came in, surprised Axel was asleep in the hammock still and that Saber had kicked off a cloak and the blankets were half off the bed although she was trembling. Dom pulled the blankets up and rewrapped her up tightly and set the cloth on her head. Saber didn't wake up when he moved the blankets, showing how bad her fever really was considering if you even stepped into a room she would have woken. Axel woke a few minutes later and looked to Dom, "Hey, how long you been here?"

"Not long, she was mumbling and lost most the blankets so I figured I'd let you nap and I could watch over her for a bit."

"She's not gotten any better," Axel sighed, "They were out in this storm for over two days with no food or water. They were put through hell, did the others have fevers?"

"They seemed to be fine," Dom shook his head, "Mason said they were fine just hungry but Red's cooking seemed to help them out. They slept a lot but have recuperated."

"Wonder what we are missing, she was injured but why is she the only one," Axel frowned.

"Infection maybe?" Dom asked.

"Doc checked all the injuries she had," Axel shook his head looking at her bandaged arms wondering if that were true, "Call the navy doc and our doc, see if they can get their heads together and figure it out."

"Sir," Dom moved as Axel got off the hammock and unstrung it before sitting on the chair. Mason and Hank came over with their doc and the two looked at the room that was filling with men, "You all should step outside, we are going to check her again for any injuries we might have missed."

"I'm not leaving," Hank frowned.

Axel glanced at the others in the room all of them were about to decline, "Out, if Saber found out you seen her body without her permission you won't like her punishment."

Axel shut the door after the last of the men left and leaned on the door watching. Hank leaned beside him, when the doctors checked her arms and legs they didn't find anything out of the ordinary, they kept her clothes on for the most part, only moving it aside to check without taking anything off. Her back had a deep cut that was dark red. Axel and Hank moved up to see it closely, "When did she get that?"

"It's a weird angle and jagged," the pirate doc murmured, "I've seen something similar before."

"Yeah," the navy doc frowned, "Keel haul punishments. She must have hit a ship when she went overboard."

They started working quickly to help her and piled the blankets on her again although she growled she was hot in Ruld. Hank held the blanket firmly over her, boxing her arms in the blanket, "This is for your own good. Bear with it, Saber."

"I'm burning up!" she grit her teeth as she raised her voice, he ignored it as she continued to struggle. Axel grabbed a canteen of water and gave her a drink carefully and they reapplied the cloth to her forehead. The doctors added another to the back of her neck. She calmed as their medicine they concocted kicked in.

They took care of Saber and more discussions until late again. Axel continued to care for her, that night was cold beyond reason and Saber's fever broke around midnight. She woke shivering with blankets piled on the bed. "So cold."

"Saber?" Axel asked wrapped in his cloak on the hammock he retied across the far edge of the room.

"Where am I?" she asked confused aware Axel was speaking Common with her instead of Zo.

"Captain's quarters since you had a high fever and it wouldn't break," Axel muttered getting up and moving toward her. His hand was warm as he felt her face, "Your fever finally broke it seems. How do you feel?"

"Tired and it's cold in here," she mumbled.

"Coming from the girl that has every available blanket and two cloaks," he scoffed, "You had us worried. This storm is on day five, we've been tied together with the navy ship for a day and a half."

"You think the storm will break soon?" she asked burrowing back into the blankets and shivering. Axel nodded, "Maybe tomorrow. Get some rest. I'm sure Red will make you anything you like now that you can coherently tell him what you want."

"If he has the ingredients I wouldn't mind some more home cooking," Saber mumbled her eyes drooping as she fought sleep again. Axel didn't say anything more just took the clothes that were wet off her forehead and the back of the neck and went back to his hammock. He slept better knowing she was out of the woods.

When the storm stopped, Saber was finally feeling normal. Red looked worn out when the storm ended. Axel looked at Red, "Are all those that were caught in the storm feeling better now?"

"The navy brats are good," he grinned to Saber who gave a cheeky grin, ignoring Killian's sputter at a high ranking officer being called a brat.

"You cannot call our officers brats," Killian frowned. He was stuffy and Axel and his crew consistently picked fun with him although Killian didn't seem to notice.

"It was his cooking that turned us into brats, before we leave I want Casserole a la home!" Saber fisted her hand and pounded the table surprising those that didn't know her well. Axel and those that had known her forever laughed. A la home stood for Bandit Casserole it seemed.

"Saber tooth's appetite is back, Red, you started it now!" Dom laughed.

"Challenge accepted!" Red smirked.

"We take off at dawn, we haven't moved in days, it's been far too long," Hank sighed.

"True but we needed a rest after that last fight," Mason mumbled. Their crew nearly didn't survive the attack but somehow they did and only lost two people.

"Anything else to discuss before we leave?" Axel asked Hank.

"Well you know Saber will demand you keep ingredients for Red to cook her homemade recipes but otherwise I think we covered everything," Hank chuckled.

"I gave Red those recipes so he could use them...I didn't expect him to cook so much for me but it's only to my benefit," Saber grinned.

"You sure we can't trade and you stay with us?" Axel asked Saber seriously, shocking the navy crew, they all growled just like pirates showing they weren't happy with that comment. Killian looked around in surprise as it was a tense standoff on the decks staring each other down.

"Stand down," Saber's voice rang in the chilly but calm air, the storm had only broke an hour ago and the two crews had gotten along so well until now.

"She's our Combatant Commander," Mason chuckled patting Dom's shoulder, "She's not joining a pirate crew."

"You never know, we have Red," Dom gave a dangerous smile back and Mason lost the smile instantly.

"I'll stay with my own crew, thanks for the offer but I'm not sure you could handle me on your crew," Saber smiled, "If I get a wild hair, a mid-life crisis, or something to that effect I'll be sure to let you know."

Axel knew she couldn't accept but wanted to offer just in case, "The offer will always stand, Saber."

They ate a final meal together and both crews were shocked when Saber hugged a few on the pirate crew and even Axel received a kiss on the cheek as she whispered, "Thanks for the save, Axel, I think I owe you a few now."

Axel couldn't correct her since she jumped to the navy deck and Mason made orders to push off. They were heading in opposite directions again. Saber glanced over to see their ship in the distance, she waved from the stern and watched as Axel raised a hand in farewell. She hoped they would have no problems as they explored and found each other on the last island.

The first island was wild untamed forest, no humans lived there. They explored for a day, Saber led the group and found plants that she couldn't identify along with some they were familiar with. Saber was surprised to find animals that were pretty dangerous, cat like animals with razor sharp teeth and black spots on their yellow fur. They found water and noted information about the islands animals before going back to the ship.

Three weeks after they found the first island, the second island was quiet with three villages on it. Saber lead one of the teams while Mason moved the ship around to the opposite side of the island. Saber didn't say anything as she got back on although she brought back a map that had four other islands on it that weren't on the one they got from Ilz. She asked Killian why a map wouldn't have islands that were easily seen while traveling between the two on the original map but he didn't have a confident answer so didn't answer at all.

One was between the third and fourth islands so they planned to stop there. The villages bartered and spoke common although they struggled with it. Saber listened to the native languages and found they were a mash of Ilz and Lidsing. She was picking it up although it was rough. The team with her were surprised as she spoke with natives. Saber wrote notes on everything they were finding to go along with the map Killian was working on. She explained the terrain and where she found water sources as they traveled around the island. They had where every village was located on the second island.

The third island only had one village and it was similar to the second island. Saber talked to Killian about the next island, "If this island is within view of the third and fourth islands why wouldn't it be on the map from Ilz?"

"Not sure," Killian rubbed his head as they sat on the stern deck talking, "Some keep them off because they are protected like our training island. Other times it is because it is too dangerous and has no resources. It could be any reason since we are in unknown waters."

"Then we will be careful," Saber muttered, the island was off their port bow and she moved to the longboat. Four people went with her, they went to search and Saber froze seeing something that caused her soul to tremble. Cannibalism was unheard of in their world. She whispered to the group, "Get back to the ship without a single noise. We have to hurry. Keep to the path we took here to avoid the traps."

The men nodded without a word, all of them were openly sweating having seen the same thing. Saber brought up the rear and when they came to the beach they stopped seeing the islanders looking over their longboat. The ship had posted watchers on deck to make sure if there were troubles to report to Hank. Saber led their group around to a rocky outcrop sitting out into the bay. Saber waved her arms to gain their attention and saw Mason running to the front and repeating her motions. She made an 'X' meaning not to come closer there was danger. She glanced back to see the villagers had noticed them and were pulling bows.

"Swim for it!" she pointed to the ship and they dove into the bay and started swimming fast. Saber pulled her sword and came back toward the beach, she wouldn't risk their men. She swiped arrows out of the air like it was nothing. She killed the islanders, five total although two were killed by arrows their comrades shot, she pushed the longboat off the beach and pulled it toward the ship. The four climbed over the side as she got close to them and helped her row. When they got to the ship they came up and Mason asked why Saber didn't try to negotiate with them.

"Take off now!" she growled not answering, "We will talk when we are clear of the bay!"

Mason wasn't used to her looking so spooked. He gave orders fast as Hank studied the two, "Alright Saber, what's wrong?"

"It wasn't on the map because the village we found were eating human beings," she told Killian, "This is what I know about the island but we didn't risk sticking around to really look it over."

She gave her report and Killian made a red X and added the meaning to the map legend, "So if we can assume that's why the other three are on the one map and not the other then I'm for skipping the other three."

"Agreed," Hank nodded, "Luckily they aren't anywhere near where we are headed so we have no reason to look them over."

"We were lucky that they were eating when we found the village," Saber shook her head, "That could have been a disaster."

"True," Mason sighed as they cleared the island and found the fourth just ahead. Saber looked to Hank three islands in a day was a little much. They didn't fly any identification on their ship in case they came across pirates or any naval military. Saber sat on the deck near the others and sighed, "That wasn't something I wanted to see. That was freaky."

"Looks like a ship is aiming right for the fourth island, let's go too," Hank murmured.

"This one is pretty big, do we want to map it like the others?" Mason asked.

"Yes but be careful," Hank met Saber's eyes. She pulled her swords and cleaned them off as they followed the other ship. When they landed they found three pirate ships with black jolly rogers. Mason was to go toward the east and around, Saber was to go on land to the west and meet on the south of the island. They would map the outside edge of the island. Saber agreed and before they even got off the ship they hit a snag. Saber was about to come down off the ship when the plank landed on the dock but instead ten men came up and stopped at the very edge of the ship.

"State your business," the Lidsing language was more prominent but still mixed with Ilz. Saber translated to Hank in Ruld.

"Tell him we are just adventurers," Hank told her quietly.

She did and he frowned grabbing her arm, "You are the only one with this mark. Were you taken from your crew on the Ax-Galley?"

"What? No," Saber frowned confused. Hank stepped closer asking what was being said and she translated quickly that these guys must have ran into Axel.

"Your tattoo is very decorative and only one crew has it that I know," the man grabbed her arm to look at the tattoo, "Shipmates die with the ship so you have to be their crew and stolen from them."

"No!" Saber shook her head, "We are friends with Captain Axel and his crew. I'm just a friend."

The word friend didn't seem to register. The man did something that looked like squid ink but once it touched her, she passed out. He must have had a fruit power or something. She woke to the waves rocking the boat. She frowned feeling as though she was off balance as she walked to the door. Saber went to grab her swords just in case but they were missing. She touched the latch at the door to open it but found it was locked. It wasn't her room or her ship it seemed. She wasn't sure where she was or what was happening. She frowned as she sat patiently. The door unlatched to let someone in and Saber found the man who asked a lot of questions without listening to the answers.

"Where's my crew?" Saber said softly in the mash of Ilz and Lidsing.

Saber studied him as he sat meeting her gaze, "Your real crew is heading to the central island, we are meeting him there to deliver you to him."

"The crew you took me from what happened to them?" Saber frowned.

"Knocked out in the harbor, what was the word you used to explain who they were," he cocked his head, "We let them live because you seemed attached to them."

"Why would that matter to pirates?" Saber asked seriously.

"We owe the Ax-Galley crew," he shrugged, "That's all you need to know. If you want to stretch your legs you can do so however you will be monitored and locked in here of a night."

"Where are my swords," she wasn't about to 'stretch her legs' without some protection.

"Do I have your word you won't use them on my crew?" he must have been the captain, she watched him. He was older and had a scar down the side of his face.

"If they don't threaten me, I won't threaten them," she finally said, "Deal?"

He nodded, "You speak this language well, the Ax-Galley spoke Common and a language close to our own but not exactly."

Saber sighed, "To us this language is a combination of two languages so it's guessing which words you might recognize."

"I see so your use of the word," he said friend in Lidsing, "That is a word from one of the two languages yet we do not understand it."

"Yes," she said as she followed him out and accepted her belt that held the two swords and a knife. She looked around to find most the crew had stopped to stare at her. Her stomach growled angrily and the captain chuckled, "Come."

They went down to the main deck and ate with the crew who were quiet watching her. She asked the captain, "How long before we meet up with Ax-Galley?"

"A week," he agreed.

She moved to the stern to look back as if she could see Hank and the others back there, the wind blew hard but at least it wasn't as cold here. Her cloak kept most the air off her. Saber glanced at the crew wondering what the heck was going on.

"Why take me just to return me to Axel?" she wondered to herself in Ruld.

The captain looked back at her, "What was that?"

"Why take me to them? You are pirates, why go out of your way?" she frowned.

He laughed, the whole crew laughed, when they calmed down the captain's first mate told her, "They saved us, of course we would go out of our way. We might be pirates but we aren't going to spit in the face of something like that."

Saber didn't say anything more. She wasn't sure if she completely trusted them but she couldn't do anything until she got to land again. She kept to herself for the most part during the week, the only time she really asked the crew any questions was when she saw their maps. They had the island that had cannibals on their map. She pointed it out and looked to the navigator, "You ever been there?"

He glanced at the captain who nodded once to answer her question and let her see the map, "No, they hunt people. If you have a map with these islands in blue that means you will be hunted."

"We landed there and found that out for ourselves," she mumbled, "The map from our home country didn't show them. We found them on a map on this island and decided to stop. We nearly didn't figure it out in time and ended up getting off the island before anyone was hurt."

They stared at her in shock, "You survived landing on that island?"

"Yeah," she cocked her head curiously.

"You didn't hit any traps?" the captain stared at her.

"I grew up as a bandit. Traps are my bread and butter," Saber shrugged looking back at the map and memorizing it.

"Hm," the captain muttered, "It's on the way, we need to make a pit stop then."

"What do you mean pit stop?" Saber repeated the phrase but didn't understand it.

"We had a run in with a group of land pirates who stole something we need to continue our travels. We were looking to get another one...ah by liberating yours but you didn't have one either. We searched after knocking you all out."

"What is it?" she frowned.

"A stone that will lead to an island. We hid our treasure on the island but those bandits took the stone from us when we were resupplying in their territory."

She frowned, land pirates meant bandits in Lidsing but they used Ilz and Lidsing words interchangeably and sounded like curse words to these pirates. Saber met his gaze, "Fine but you owe me one."

"Sure," he smiled, "I'll give you a detailed map of the known world."

"This isn't all of it?" she frowned looking at the map.

"Nope," the navigator grinned, "Why would we have the full map out when we need a specific area."

Saber didn't think about that, their maps were different and had more accurate navigator information than their own known world. She looked to the captain, "Fine but I want all the detailed ones of the known world along with it."

"Fine," he nodded.

They went toward the island and Saber realized they were bypassing the meeting place where Axel and Hank agreed to meet. She looked at the navigator, "On the way my ass."

He grinned, "It's worth it."

Chapter 7

Saber was to stay with the captain and his first mate when they landed on the island, she wasn't to take off but she found Dom sitting at a table near the docks. "Dom!"

Saber jumped the waist high fence and hugged him and then seen Axel, she hugged him too, "What are you two doing here?"

"The question is why are you here?" Axel pulled back to study her. She looked tired with dark circles under her eyes. Every time he seen her, she looked tired with dark bags like that. He wondered why this time. He stood with Dom prepared for anything.

"We got blindsided by these guys, they knocked the whole crew out and took me because they recognized the tattoo," she nodded toward her arm, "I wasn't sure what to think until I saw you guys."

"Leo," Axel met the other captain's eyes angry that they would pull a stunt like that and cause Saber so much stress, "Stealing Saber from her crew is not good."

"We assumed wrong," Leo shrugged, "She's safe although I'd like to keep her for a while yet."

"Keep her?" Axel raised an eyebrow, "If anyone is laying claim, then she's mine."

Axel's arm wrapped around her shoulders. Saber looked up at him in surprise, "I...I'm laying claim to myself, don't make me slap you two idiots."

Her fast Zo made Leo cock his head but Axel chuckled, "Calm down, Saber, people on this side of the world see women as objects to own.

They stole you back because you wear our mark. Girls aren't fighters here."

Saber looked up at him, "I'll forgive you if you have Red cook me Bandit Delight. I haven't had the greatest trip and I'm not in the mood to be owned or otherwise claimed."

Axel squeezed her shoulders, "Sure, Red is getting provisions now."

Saber looked to Leo, "He wants to get some kind of rock from the bandits who are around here."

"Bandits huh? What does he know about you, Saber?" Axel frowned instantly.

"I asked about the islands in blue, the islands in blue means people hunt and eat other people there and to avoid them. We didn't know that and stopped at one. Luckily, we figured that out before anyone was hurt just before running into them at the next island a few hours later. When I brought it up, they asked how we avoided falling into their traps on the island and I told them I grew up as a bandit."

"A rock?" Dom asked her.

She nodded, "He said it leads to another island. That's why they attacked our crew was to see if we had a rock but we didn't. He took me and said he left the crew on the island passed out on the ship."

"Leo you weren't lying to Saber were you?" Axel met his gaze, "That crew she was with is like family to us. No one was hurt or killed?"

"No, they were all knocked out and left on their ship with five uninjured to make sure no one else came after them although we tied them up while we searched the ship," Leo murmured.

Saber didn't hear any lies but languages and cultures made it difficult to truly gauge if they were honest or understand their fast thoughts. If she knew the languages better and not the mishmash of Ilz and Lidsing she would feel better. They had traveled a good distance away from where she had seen Axel last and it had warmed up. She didn't wear the cloak since it was warm like a desert heat.

Leo explaining to Axel what they needed back from the bandits. Ruld thoughts caught her attention, she frowned looking around, she slowed as they walked, Axel glanced down still having an arm around her shoulders. "What's wrong, Saber?"

"I hear Ruld thoughts," she mumbled, "Not just any Ruld thoughts they are in my dialect from the mountains area."

"How is that even possible?" Dom frowned at her.

"I don't know," she shook her head, "I can tell it's male but it's impossible to narrow down."

"What are they thinking?" Axel asked curiously.

"Don't notice or I'll slit your throat," she mumbled to Dom, "They are stealing something."

"Well it is a town filled with cutthroats and bandits," Dom shrugged.

"True," Axel agreed. They walked for a few more minutes, Leo talking to them and Saber distracted by the idea of someone from Ruld being there.

She noticed someone was preparing to go after Red's purse which was tucked inside his breeches, she knew from watching him in markets before where he hid it. She left Axel's side, and called, "Red step to your right and give me a hug!"

Red's head jerked up as he obeyed instantly. Her authoritative voice had been pounded into his head from her training him all those years ago. She hugged him quickly with a grin and froze seeing the man look at her angrily.

"Bravo?" she looked stunned as she asked quickly in Ruld, "Is that you?"

"Who are you?" the man frowned looking her over. The Ruld language caused her to think her father had lied and her brother had somehow lived.

Saber froze, if it were her brother then he would recognize her even though she had grown, her face hadn't changed much over the years, "Saber."

"Saber what?" he growled his knife flashing in the sun as he turned to face them. Saber pushed Red back when he started to step between them.

"It's fine, Red," she growled in Zo before switching to Ruld, "Now answer me, who are you if you aren't Bravo?"

"How do you know Bravo?" he searched her face.

"You first!" Saber grit her teeth.

He stepped back away from them, still eyeing them as he pulled his shirt up and turned, "Bravo is my younger brother."

"You...it can't be..." Saber looked stunned, "A...Ace?"

"Now tell me how you know my brother!" Ace attacked fast and hard. She wasn't talking and could be an enemy for all he knew. He planned to force her to talk if she wouldn't the easy way. Saber dodged it without pulling her swords.

"Saber," Axel warned seeing the man she assumed was Ace had two knives.

"Don't get involved," Saber shook her head, "This is personal."

Dom sighed leaning on the wall watching. Axel and Red as well although Leo and his first mate were staring in shock as she dodged attack after attack. She detected a thought too fast to understand but the intent was animalistic and close. She was a step ahead of Dom's shout of warning that someone was attacking from behind her. She rolled forward twisting to bring Ace to the ground and she stood turning to the new threat. It was a move that Bravo had taught her when she was six years old and she broke her wrist when he did it to her and she wasn't ready to land. Ace however recovered fast and was back on his feet. Saber saw the sword the one man carried and four others prepared for anything.

"Friends of yours…Ace?" she asked with a grin.

"How do you know my name?" he swiped at her again but she caught his wrist and met his gaze, "You were taken from the village when you were around eight years old."

He froze and raised his other hand toward the men about to jump in. Saber let him walk around and lift her shirt to see the tattoo. He let it drop and stepped back around to study her. "I don't remember a girl with your name."

"Probably because a few months after you were taken I was born," she met his gaze, "Maybe I should introduce myself…I'm Saber Aldara Barca youngest daughter to Saul Barca."

"How are you here?" he searched her face and then shook his head, "You look like mom."

He gave a fascinated smirk as he studied her. Saber glanced at his friends, "Well I guess that's a long story. Your friends don't look too keen on waiting for me to explain all that much."

"Are you staying here somewhere?"

"I'm with the ship in port," she nodded toward Axel who Ace looked over curiously.

"Pirates huh?"

"Well considering that's part of the story," Saber shook her head.

"I'll come to the docks in two hours, I have to take care of business first."

"Do you have a rock?" Saber asked before he turned toward his men, "Something about a rock leading to an island or something I don't quite understand. It's how I landed here."

"Yeah but it does me no good, you want the rock then I want something in return," he met her gaze, "I want a map of the other side of the known world...where Ruld is on the map."

She cocked her head for a second and glanced at Axel before nodding, "If that's it then sure."

He studied her for another minute, "I cannot believe after all these years I finally found a piece of home."

Saber motioned to his friends, "Hurry up, I have some fast talking to do."

Ace looked to Axel and frowned, "You mess with her and I'll kill you."

His announcement made Axel raise an eyebrow but not say a word. Saber sighed aggravated that even though he never met her it was a repeat of Bravo's attitude of protectiveness all over again. She stepped to the group and said, "Enough excitement can we find a bath house and go back to your ship please?"

"We have a shower on the ship," Axel told her, "No bathhouses here...or I should clarify...these bathhouses are mixed gender."

"I'll just steal your shower thanks so much," she muttered as they turned to head down the street. Axel glanced back to see Ace studying them. Saber didn't look back but up at him, "You alright with a guest?"

"To the ship?" he cocked his head, "Who that jerk?"

"Can Red make Bandit's Delight for him too?" she asked Axel seriously, "Please Axel?"

"Who the hell is that guy?" Dom growled, "You were fighting and then all the sudden so chummy."

"I've never met him before today but..." Saber ducked her head for a minute before smiling to Dom and Axel both, "He's my oldest brother Ace."

"What?" Dom frowned, "You said your brother was stolen from the village before you were born."

"He was," Saber nodded.

"He had the RNB tattoo," Red told Dom who hadn't seen what he showed Saber and Red when she cut in on Ace's attempt to steal Red's purse.

"Sure, Saber but what did you ask him before he left?" Axel sighed.

"If he had Leo's rock," Saber shrugged.

"And?" Dom asked curiously.

"He said yes and he'd give it to me but in return he wants a map of our side of the world...showing Ruld."

"I see," Axel nodded, "Dom have a map prepared then. Leo wants a damn rock then I want to see why."

"Thanks Axel," Saber met his gaze.

Axel smirked, "I'm in the mood for bandit delight so it's no trouble for one more mouth to feed."

Saber stopped and bought clothes so she had clean clothes after her shower although the clothes were weird to her. Axel paid since she was taken from her ship. She studied him as they walked to the ship, "Why are you staring at our captain, Saber?"

Dom's voice told her that he was smiling. Saber caught Axel's eyes swivel to meet hers. She sighed, "I think when we catch back up to Captain Hank that I need to settle up my debts. Seriously you save me from a storm, now this, and not to mention buying clothes and the list goes on."

"We owed you for saving Bentley remember? Not to mention the other 50 or so kids from the village," Axel met her gaze, "We still owe you, Saber. So don't go thinking you are repaying a debt and sending us further into your debt understand."

She frowned confused and Dom laughed, "You have no idea what he means do you?"

"Anthony was my student so of course I had to help him with those bandits...no debt for that," Saber frowned.

"We agree to disagree then," Axel muttered as they got to the ship and those that were guarding were shocked to find Saber with them.

Saber took Axel's room and enjoyed a shower. She was surprised the shirts for women were so short. They didn't reach her waistband of her breeches. She came out with wet hair and sat on the stern deck with Dom, Axel, and Leo although she didn't like Leo's gaze on her skin. She sat next to Axel and wrapped her arms around her legs as they talked, effectively hiding her torso and cleavage. Leo left soon enough and it was quiet as Hunter worked on the map. Anthony called that they had a guest. Saber turned to see her brother studying Anthony.

"Come up," Axel motioned as Dom stood and watched him. Anthony moved out of his way and Ace came up to the stern deck.

"Axel...Dom...meet Ace Barca," Saber introduced in common.

"Nice to meet you," Dom greeted sitting with him.

"Same," Ace murmured, "So I guess you wanted this?"

The rock was the size of Saber's hand, she looked to Axel who studied it for a long moment. "Yes that's what Leo was looking for."

"It leads to an island that floats on the ocean currents and never stays in one place," Ace explained, "Many pirates use that island to hide their treasures or hide and rest."

"I see," Dom looked at it surprised.

"Supper is done," Red announced bringing a huge tray up and serving the four of them bandit's delight. Ace took a bite and froze. Saber was shocked that tears threatened to spill out of his eyes when he looked to Red.

"You...how do you know how to make this?" he asked shocked.

"Tastes just like home, right?" Saber asked him seriously.

"Did you give him the recipe?" Ace frowned.

"Yeah," Saber didn't deny it.

He fell silent and ate it all. When he finished he looked to Red, "Thanks, to be honest it's been over 24 years since I had Bandit's Delight or any RNB dishes."

"So how did you get here from RNB?" Dom asked curiously.

"Lidsing scum stole me and about ten other kids. From RNB we were marched for what felt like forever in chains to the coast. I was sold to a ship as a cabin boy on a pirate ship. They made a mistake landing on an island with odd eating habits. Most were killed but I made a run for it and found another ship coming into the bay, I stopped them although there was a language barrier. They kept me on their ship for a month and then dropped me off here. Said I was too young."

"So you are with the bandits here?"

"Stick with what you know," he flashed an amused smile at Saber who had asked him, "They were all dropped off here for whatever reason and now it's our island, we run the show."

"You the head honcho then?" Dom asked him surprised.

"For the most part, although there are two others that share responsibility over the city with me. So you said it's a long story, start at the beginning, Saber, I want to hear everything."

"Everything?" she glanced to the guys and down at the finished bowl of delight.

"You thought I was Bravo, did you get split up from him or was he taken too?" Ace asked seriously.

Saber started at the very beginning and Ace sat shocked to find that Saber was the only survivor of the family. He stared at her for a long moment as she moved into the story of traveling Ruld, surviving in the woods and stealing. Giselle and Ulric Thompson taking her in and joining the navy. How they sent her to Axel to train under him in dual swords and their story. Then how the years passed and being assigned to travel this side of the world in hopes of mapping the entire world. Saber then explained how the journey had been for her so far with pirates and getting abducted from her ship and brought here by Leo. Ace looked to Axel, "So you are friends with this captain although you are in the navy?"

"Yeah," she nodded.

"I'd love to go home, I never met a ship from Lidsing after the pirates died on that island," Ace sighed leaning back, "Never a dull moment and you have a nickname in the navy?"

"Saber tooth Tiger," Dom chuckled since he was the one that mentioned it before, "She's lethal and everyone knows not to mess with her."

"Dom," she shook her head but Axel nodded in agreement when Ace looked to him.

"So are you staying with these pirates until you meet up with this Captain Hank character?" Ace asked curiously.

"That was the plan," Saber sighed, "I had a rough few days so resting up is best."

Axel smirked, "We wouldn't let her risk finding a different ship. Not with the culture around here toward women so horrible."

"True," Ace agreed knowing how women were treated.

"So where was Hank when you were abducted, Saber?" Axel asked.

"He had two more islands to map after the fourth where Leo took me," Saber sighed. They talked about where they had been and what they had seen. Axel was surprised when Leo came back over and had a copy of the known world with in-depth maps of specific regions for Saber. He asked if she was ready to barter and seeing the maps, Axel was shocked he hadn't asked for that as well. Saber agreed and Dom set the rock they wanted on the table. Hunter had cut off a decent chunk, cut it again for Saber to have a piece, and tucked it away well before Leo arrived. "All the maps for the rock."

"Of course," Leo agreed. Axel had Hunter look at the region specific to where they were now and he agreed it was correct as Saber did the same for the region she had seen. Axel accepted the maps for her and Dom handed the stone over. Leo thanked them before he left with his ship back toward where they had come. Axel told Hunter to copy all the maps so that Saber could keep one and they had a copy. Ace studied them, finding that Saber was comfortable with them without knowing what hell most girls went through on the island.

"I need to get back, will you be here tomorrow?"

"We leave after restocking our supplies," Axel told him, "We should be done with that by dawn."

"I see."

"If you want to travel with us then be on the boat at dawn," Axel told him.

Ace was shocked but didn't say anything as he left. Saber watched him leave, "You would really let him travel with you?"

"Not being able to go home for that long," Axel shook his head, "I can't even imagine that."

Saber relaxed as they sat on the ship, Axel and Dom talking with the other officers. Saber started to fall asleep and ended up leaning on Axel who studied her in surprise. Ace slipped back to the ship late that night to ask Axel a few questions, glancing around for Saber.

"Where's my sister?" Ace asked confused.

"Sleeping," Axel murmured, "What did you want?"

"You invited me on the ship but...I have two children and when you are a bandit, you stay a bandit until the day you die. I will have to disappear carefully to avoid getting killed but I can't do that if I have to leave the twins behind."

"How old are they?" Axel asked quietly.

"Twelve," Ace rubbed his head.

"They'll have to work to earn their keep but they can come along," Axel murmured, "How can I deny Saber from meeting her brother's children?"

"Thanks Axel, I'll be back close to dawn with the kids," he murmured.

"The tide changes at 4am, we will leave as soon as you board."

Ace turned and disappeared.

Chapter 8

Saber slept until well after dawn, she came out with her hair down, stretching up ignoring that the clothes she bought rode up. She froze seeing they were already at sea. "Morning sleepyhead," Axel greeted behind her.

"Ace?" she asked looking back at him.

"He's here and he brought a surprise," Axel told her stepping to her.

"Saber!" Anthony called, "Come teach us some more."

"Fine but I want food after," Saber sighed with a tolerant smile glancing to Axel, "He wants his butt whooped."

Axel smirked and leaned on the railing. She fought Anthony and then turned and told a few of the younger boys to come at her, three against one and she was still winning. Axel shook his head watching her using her power to avoid the attacks from behind. He heard a young girl's voice, "Who is that, da?"

"That is Saber," Ace murmured.

"She has the same tattoo as you," the boy said moving to stand between Axel and his sister, protective since they grew up knowing the danger to girls and his twin was his top priority.

Saber was giving instructions as she dodged attack after attack. Dom finally bellowed, "Alright you children enough! Time for the big boys to play!"

The officers all went round after round with her. She fought with them, keeping it polite although they all were holding back. Axel sighed, "I need to exercise or I'll get fat myself."

"What?" the twins turned to look up at him.

"A captain has to show he is capable too," Axel flashed a smile standing on the railing about to jump down as he looked over all their heads, "Saber you too tired to have one more round?"

"Bring it on," Saber turned to look up at him. He jumped down and accepted two wooden swords from two officers who only fought with one each. He attacked without warning, Saber skipped back to avoid the side-swipe from the left. Her shirt was slowly riding up and she was being careful so it didn't show too much skin. He continued to fight, getting a full blown workout but still holding back. Saber grinned as he continued, not giving her time to fix her shirt. "Captain Axel are you trying to give your men a show too?"

"I thought you were going to give me a workout at least," he flashed an amused smile. She raised a finger and he paused as she tugged the shirt down as far as she could and glanced around, "I need a hair tie."

She was surprised a young girl tossed it down from above, she was smiling but Saber was surprised there were young children onboard. She tied her hair up and her shirt rode up again. "If I show more than this we stop, understand, captain?"

"Of course," he grinned as she left it alone and attacked hard and fast. They were going full out and the crew moved back to give even more room. Axel wasn't holding anything back and Saber was playing dirty with everything she had. She wanted to know how she stacked up against him after so many years. She winced when the wooden sword hit her leg. She backflipped away and lounged instantly back to him. He barely slid to the side, her sword catching his shirt and ripping it. He noticed she was open and used his elbow to hit her shoulder pushing her to the ground. She swiped her legs around hitting him to the ground and landed on his chest having lost her sword.

He grabbed her legs and yanked her around until he had her pinned and Saber breathing fast said, "I concede, Axel, give me your shirt right now."

"What?" he asked breathing fast as well.

"Shirt, now!" she growled.

He pulled his shirt off and she slipped it on before anyone could see that her shirt's seam ripped up the side and her breastband was the only thing keeping her from exposing everything from the waist up. She let him help her up and her shirt fell to the ground at her feet. She grabbed it and he raised an eyebrow, "I apologize for undressing you in front of my men."

"You have a nail loose," she raised the oversized shirt up to show a cut on her side, the shipwrights moved forward to fix it immediately as she moved to walk past Axel who caught her shoulder and called the doc to put a balm on it. Saber looked up at Axel and said, "For seven years I have learned all kinds of things so I was stronger...I guess I still have room to grow."

"What's that mean?" Axel looked surprised, "You nearly had me at least six times by my count."

"Eight," Dom corrected, "We were about to step in since it was getting dangerous."

Saber looked to Dom, "And how many times did Axel nearly have me?"

"Nine," another officer murmured.

"You see," Saber poked Axel's side and happened to look down to see he was ripped and had a few scars. The doc finished and Saber ripped her eyes away from Axel who hadn't noticed since he was looking at the cut being wrapped by the doc. She went to change her shirt and brought his shirt back to him, the shirt she had bought was a tube top which irritated her, "Next port, I need real clothes."

She complained as she came out the door. Axel looked surprised as she handed the shirt to him. Her tattoo was on show at her back, three huge scars were seen as well and before he could say anything, he put his shirt on and the little girl appeared near them. "What's the scars from?"

"What?" Saber turned to look down at her, "Who are you? Don't tell me Axel had a love child hidden away on the ship."

The officers all roared with laughter as Axel made a face, "No!"

"I'm Salah and my twin is Sebastian," the girl said, "And our da is Ace Barca."

Saber studied the girl in shock but blinked, "What scars are you asking about?"

She moved to sit on the deck watching others exercising as they continued on their journey. "This one," Salah touched her shoulder where the scar went down to her collarbone.

"That...a pirate captain decided to cut down his own man and got me in the shoulder."

"What about this one?" she asked touching the one that wrapped around her arm.

"That...a whip an enemy used to catch people and yank them closer to swipe at them."

"And this one?" she asked touching her side.

"A fight I don't remember...he was called a giant," Saber looked down.

"Da said only people who have fought to protect those they love get a tattoo like this," Sebastian said squatting behind her studying it.

"That is true," Ace sat close to them, "I just got my tattoo when I was taken from home."

"So you were eight?" Saber asked surprised.

"Yeah when did you get it?" Ace frowned watching the men.

"Seven. I was the youngest to receive it of the siblings," she murmured.

"Da said he had brothers but who are you?" Sebastian frowned as he sat on Ace's free side studying Saber around his dad.

"Kids this is my sister," Ace murmured, "Your Aunt."

"Aunt Saber?" Salah asked surprised.

"I wasn't born before your dad was taken from our village," Saber braced her arms leaning back with a sigh, "I met him yesterday for the first time."

"So you got yours at a younger age?" Sebastian pressed going back to the tattoo.

"My da forced me to get it when I was seven for protecting my friends," she glanced to Ace who didn't seem to want to tell his kids what the tattoo meant just yet.

"Pirates ahead!" the crows nest yelled. Everyone put the practice weapons away and prepared. Saber grabbed the black sheathes at her waist as she stood, Axel touched her shoulder, "Let's see what happens, I'm not really in the mood to pick a fight."

They were quiet as the ship continued to move past without any attention to them. Saber turned to follow their ship with her eyes. *Keep going, we'll see you tonight.*

Axel studied her eyes, "You okay, Saber?"

"Night raid," she mumbled, "We need to get away from here, are we changing direction anytime soon?"

"We weren't planning on it," Axel glanced back to see the ship continuing, "What did you hear?"

Saber told him quietly and he nodded, "Good to know."

They continued to go, Axel quietly told the officers who prepared everyone else. Ace knew something was up but the kids were oblivious and Saber distracted them as best as possible.

Late that night Saber had the twins in her room who were sleeping in the hammock and bed, she sat at the table in the dark waiting. The door opened, and the noise level escalated to a roar. The twins woke as Saber fought the man who stormed in. She killed him and kicked him out of the room. She shut the door back and barred it again. Salah and Sebastian sat motionless, "What's going on?"

"The ship we passed this afternoon decided to come back to attack us now," Saber told them, "Be silent and don't move."

Salah moved to sit with Sebastian and then they didn't move at all. The door was kicked in and three men came in. Saber killed two and the third was proving to have some kind of power that caused her some trouble. She heard a call from outside, "Saber you good?"

Axel had called and she called back, "I have a power type, don't count on me to help until he's gone."

Her opponent scoffed but she attacked hard and fast, the power only worked some of the time so she attacked faster and faster. Her blades seemed to be a blur in the darkened room. She hit harder and harder until she pressed him back, he tripped over one of the fallen men on the ground and Saber dodged his lounge to slam her sword into his chest. She had taken damage, but seeing the three were dead she risked a glance back, the twins had moved off the hammock and were pressed into the corner of the room.

"You two aren't hurt are you?" she asked checking the three to make sure they weren't just injured but truly dead.

"We are fine," Sebastian said his arms around his sister watching Saber.

"Good," She grabbed one of the men and tossed him out the door. She did the same to the other two. She called loud enough for Axel to hear her, "All clear in here, Axel. How's it looking out there?"

"They seem to be set to play last man standing," Dom's voice sounded closer to her, "Are you sure you want to stay in or come out for some fun?"

"I couldn't take all your fun, Dom," Saber knew Salah was scared.

"We will be okay if you need to go outside," Sebastian murmured.

"No," Saber grinned, "I'm having fun with the idiots who are targeting this room."

Two more came in, one had a hat on that she recognized from meeting Leo, it had to be a culture thing for the unknown world where captains wore specific hats. She looked at the other and frowned, "Who are you?"

"First mate," the other grinned pulling a sword.

"Leave now, before I decide you will leave when you draw your last breathe," Saber glared.

"Come now," the captain grinned looking her over, "Don't make us harm your beautiful skin or punish you by killing your children."

Saber pressed them back, out the door, and found Axel and Dom there to cut them off from her, cutting into her fight. She grabbed Dom's shoulder, "You protect the kids, I'll be back in a moment. That one is mine."

Dom skipped back to avoid the sword the captain had swiped at him. Saber had a look he had never seen before in her eyes. He stepped back and shut the door staying in the room with the twins. Saber shocked those that saw her fighting on the moonlit deck, the captain didn't stand a chance. She cut in on Axel's fight and he stepped back to the door to protect from the outside since that's where the entire crew of enemy pirates were aiming. Saber killed the first mate and captain and jumped onto the railing, "I killed your captain and first mate. Leave before I slaughter you all!"

They continued to fight but were retreating. Saber pulled her knife when one tried to rally his friends to keep fighting. She threw it hard and it slammed into his throat. Everyone froze having heard him calling and sudden silence. She had both swords in one hand since she threw the knife. "I won't tell you again. Don't think I will be lenient."

They retreated but as they had been fighting the cannons had been aimed and hit the enemy ship over and over to the point, they wouldn't make it very far without getting to a port for repairs. Unlike Saber, Axel told them to attack the mast and other vital points.

Saber found that all of them had retreated and their ship was starting to lag behind them. She got to the door and tapped, "Dom, open the door."

Dom came out, his sword still out same as the rest of the crew. She looked in at the twins, "You two alright?"

"Yeah," Salah was shaken.

Axel was on the roof watching their hasty retreat, "Their mast just fell. We are clear."

"Good," Saber took the clothe from Dom to clean her swords, putting them up and looking at the twins seeing they were staring at her, "You can come out, it's safe now."

They slipped out and Ace was hugged. The doctor looked Saber over and wrapped the few cuts and scrapes she had. The crew was studying her as she looked at the twins. "What happened, Saber?" Ace asked.

"No one threatens me or those I want to protect," Saber met his gaze, her eyes were still ice cold.

"You have the same look in your eyes as our da used to when he got angry," Ace was surprised, "What happened?"

"It's fine, I just lost my temper."

"I'd say, you cut into my fight," Axel frowned at her.

"Excuse me, captain, but you cut into my fight without asking. Dom too," she turned to look up at him, "The door to your room is broken."

"Can you deal with it for a night?" he asked her glancing down at her niece, "I'm sorry Salah but it seems you and your aunt will have to sleep with the door open tonight."

"It's okay," Salah stepped to Saber looking up at her, "Is that what it means to protect people to get the tattoo you and dad have?"

Sebastian looked up at Ace who studied his sister, he had seen the last of the fight when she stepped out of the room. He was on the deck at the prow and had seen her fight like a demon, he was stunned to find that the exercise that afternoon looked like nothing compared to her fight with the enemies on the deck. She sighed softly, "Protecting those you care about. Come on, I'm tired Salah. Is Sebastian staying in the room as well?"

Sebastian looked to Saber and nodded. They cleaned the room quickly and then Saber laid on the bed ignoring the twins who were quietly settling down. "Aunt Saber?" Salah asked slipping on the bed behind her.

"Hm?" Saber turned to face the door, Salah at her back.

"Thanks for protecting us," she murmured.

"You are my family," Saber mumbled, "You don't have to thank me for that, Salah. Let me sleep, I'm tired."

Salah's hand gripped Saber's shirt as though she needed physical contact to sleep. Saber ignored the pressure and slept hard. Axel glanced in as he moved off the roof and studied the two, Saber lying close to the door to protect Salah from any threat that may come from outside, and Sebastian in the hammock tired and sleeping already. Dom glanced in as well seeing that Saber was peacefully sleeping as if nothing had happened.

They moved away from the door, finding Ace was at their backs as well looking at the scene, they leaned on the railing, "They have to be tired after all the excitement. Saber says she lost her temper but what the hell was that?"

Ace's voice was quiet knowing the door was broken and if Saber was anything like the rest of the family then any small noise would wake her up. Axel murmured, "I've never seen her fight like that and I thought I knew her fighting skills well having watched her for a few months now. It's like a completely different style. Maybe it was the moonlight but it wasn't the same."

"Agreed," Dom murmured, "She caught my arm in a vise grip, it's still sore. She has never stopped me like that before. If that is losing her temper then I'd hate to see her angry."

Axel watched the men clean, they all went to sleep late that night. Axel went to wake the ladies and Sebastian for breakfast. Saber cracked an eye as soon as he crossed into the room and closed it again, "Is it morning already?"

Saber's voice sounded tired still. "Yeah, Red is cooking."

"Good," Saber sighed sitting up, Axel leaned on the door watching her, she tossed her hair back up in a ponytail. Salah woke in a panic when Saber had pulled out of her grip.

"Aunt Saber?" she asked, her voice high.

"It's fine, Salah, it's time for breakfast. Captain Axel was just making sure we didn't miss it. Wake your brother."

"I'm awake," Sebastian swung his legs around to stand. Saber stood with a stretch as she stepped to Axel who let her out.

"How far away are we from a village, I need new clothes again," she made a face.

Axel chuckled, "I'll take you as soon as we get to a port, Saber."

She moved to the railing and sat feeling bruises from the night's fight, "Man that fight last night feels like half my body is bruised."

She had bruises and bandages but they could tell she was still tired. Red handed her a bowl and said, "This should help."

Saber smiled, "Thanks Red."

Axel sat with the officers and Saber; Salah, Sebastian and Ace sat nearby. Ace studied Saber out of the corner of his eyes as they all ate. Saber sighed feeling like Red had given her a week of rest, "Red's food always makes me feel better. It's amazing."

"Saber last night," Axel turned serious as the other officers stayed sitting as Red came back around to pick up the bowls, "There was a moment when you completely changed. You said you lost your temper."

"What about it?" Saber asked.

"Your fighting skills...they seemed to change," Gun said quietly watching her.

"Change how?" Saber frowned, "I told you I lost my temper. How was I different?"

"You fought with your non-dominant hand first," Axel started.

"You also seemed to have speed, faster than usual."

"I don't know about that," Saber shook her head, "I was protecting my family, they made comments that ticked me off."

The rest of their trip to the next island went without issue. Axel, as promised, went shopping for clothes with Saber who was relieved she had better clothes. They stayed there waiting for a week and a half for Hank's ship who appeared looking a little worn but not broken. The crew were shocked Saber was with them and safe.

Saber showed Hank, Mason, and Killian the maps. The end of the world wasn't in sight yet. Axel and the others had identified the end of their known world was the back of their own continent. The worry of finding the end of the world was gone. Saber asked Hank, "Do we want to stop moving this way and go out and around to see if we find if it's a sphere instead of just a loop? We would end up back in our islands between Zosha and Ruld if we went there. We might even find more islands between."

"It's been over a year already," Hank sighed, "Let's confirm the maps, we've had enough excitement on this trip. Do we want to travel together? We will start to run into Zosha ships the closer we get toward Zosha anyway."

"Sure," Axel nodded, "I'd feel better with us both traveling together. We don't know your signals though so can we keep Saber with us between islands?"

"Sure," Hank sighed seeing that his combatant commander was brushing the little girl's hair and talking to the kids.

The majority of the trip to Zosha was quiet, some ships started to aim for them but because they were traveling together the ships avoided a confrontation with them. They pulled into Axel's home port and rested for a few days. Red got more ingredients for Giselle for Saber to take home. Axel told her, "We will come visit soon, Saber."

They went to eat as her family moved to the naval ship. Saber sat with them on the edge of the city with some people she remembered from the village they started leaving one by one to see their family. When she looked up at Axel, she realized they were miraculously alone, "Axel...thank you for saving me, twice, and letting my brother and his kids travel with us."

"I'm thinking about making another trip toward Ruld. Maybe we can travel again together," Axel studied her.

"Maybe," she shocked him when she stepped toward him and went to kiss his cheek, he turned slightly and caught her lips. She stared at him in surprise, "Axel?"

"I can't talk you into staying with us, Saber?" he asked studying her.

"I...I can't be a pirate, as a bandit I lost everyone," she whispered, "As an officer in the navy I think I have a better chance at protecting those I really want to keep close. I have a family who wouldn't understand going back like that. Don't get me wrong, Axel, I really like you but I've been on that side of the law and almost lost my life. I don't have it in me to go back to risk it again."

"I understand," he murmured, "But you always have a home here as well."

"And you always have a home in Ruld," she kissed him again knowing it was like she was saying goodbye.

"We are going to report to the king tomorrow," Axel told her.

Saber nodded as they walked back to the port. She got on Hank's ship and found most of Axel's crew there on the dock, waving them off. Saber didn't move to swipe her face of tears and no one else noticed thankfully.

She had reinvigorated her contacts as she traveled back to Ruld. When they arrived they were rewarded with rank promotions and huge celebrations for four weeks straight.

Ace was introduced to Ulric and Giselle who were shocked but welcomed them like lost children and grandchildren. Giselle was doing better with Red's ingredients he had sent to her although they were almost completely out of the initial bag that Red had given to them before they went to the unknown world. Ace didn't like the ocean since that meant he'd be gone a lot. Ulric introduced him to the army branch in the port city and because of his history he became a trainer for both the army and navy. Saber went to check in on him with the twins for lunch to the army training area. A lieutenant showed them to his training area where he was teaching them and Saber smiled watching him sweating freely as he taught them. They were doing a dual training for the army and navy at the training island in a week and Saber was going. It would be her first time there since her fight with Benji the giant there.

Her communications went off and she pulled it out of her pocket as the twins looked at her in surprise. "Combatant Commander Barca."

"Saber, it's Hank, you have two hours to get in a uniform and report to HQ."

"Why?" she frowned, "We already reported everything don't tell me it's another celebration because I'm partied out sir."

"No. I won't ruin the surprise but bring your family with you because it's a big ordeal and uh…the King is involved."

Saber frowned but knew he wouldn't tell her over comms so agreed stepping into the sun to be noticed. Her brother called a break and looked over at her, "Saber? What are you doing here?"

"We need to go to the house, evidently it's an emergency."

"Okay," he frowned, "That's all for today, good work!"

They went home and got ready, Giselle and Ulric evidently were warned because they helped the twins and Ace by having clothes ready for them when they got home. Saber wore her dress uniform with all her medals feeling the weight of the medals on her chest. Salah took her hand when they met in the entryway. A carriage arrived and they all got in and went to the HQ building to the ballroom.

"What is going on, Old Man?" Saber asked as they traveled knowing he had friends still in the branches and had to have an idea.

"I'm honestly not sure," Ulric frowned as Giselle patted her hand gently. When they got out and went inside the family was shown to seats of honor near the stage as Saber was stopped just outside with Hank and the officers of the crew.

"What is going on, Cap'n?" she frowned.

"Not sure," Hank frowned, "I just know that we were all to report here in dress uniform and that our king would be in attendance."

"Great," she sighed.

They were announced as the doors opened and they saluted the king without moving. "Thank you for coming Vice Admiral Hank and your officers. Three hours ago we had a surprise delegation arrive in our port from Zosha. Duke Ridley please explain to our court what your request of us was from our royal counterpart?"

"Thank you, your majesty," Duke Ridley was a thin man with long hair tied back at his shoulders. He explained that the old king passed about eight months ago and his son was taking an active approach to revamping the kingdom. Their king requested that he would like to create a military exchange system between them. Every six months their best Naval crew would train at Ruld and the other six months Ruld's best would come to Zosha to fight. They would be at peace and have ambassadors that would stay in the other countries. Duke Ridley opened the letter the king had sent with him to mention the names of those he had heard about from Ruld that he'd like to invite to Zosha for the exchange program. Hank's crew, Saber stood shocked as she heard her specifically mentioned.

"Combatant Commander Barca has trained in Zosha in the past and the king invites her to return. As Zosha is requesting this suddenly it is requested that a letter be sent back to agree or disagree to the exchange program. If you should agree the naval ship I arrived on would stay to train under the navy here and have authority to be under contract to work in protecting Ruld's waters and I would act as the Ambassador for the six months. Another ambassador will come to stay permanently after the initial six months."

"Admiral Oliver stated that you have close ties with Zosha, Vice Admiral Hank. I would like to know about your experience with either the country or their people."

"Yes sire," Hank saluted and gave his history with traveling while protecting merchant ships. He mentioned that a Zosha ship had assisted them in mapping the unknown world. Duke Ridley listened in silence as Hank concluded, "The ship in question, the Ax-Galley saved Combatant Commander Barca on two separate occasions and that crew has my respect and full trust, sire."

"Combatant Commander Barca," the king turned his eyes to her. She saluted and held it waiting for him to continue. She spent a long time explaining her relationship with Zosha citizens, including contacts she had with merchants who sold Ruld products there year round's feedback she had received in the past. Soon it was Mason's turn to speak as well. The king looked to Duke Ridley who studied the young commanders in surprise that they were serious and the reports he had heard were just as cut and dry with nothing missing or dramatically over stated. He was surprised that almost all of it was positive.

"Based on their report we will agree to a two year trial however one change," the king murmured explaining that while a ship was in port at Ruld from Zosha, a Ruld ship would be at Zosha port at the same time with a six month change so that neither kingdom was down a ship during the six months. "Vice Admiral Hank your team will be the second ship to travel to Zosha. The first will be Captain Louis York, he's kept the border waters for nearly ten years with very little travel so for six months they will learn from Zosha and as Duke Ridley explained answer to Zosha's king any orders while protecting their waters. Vice Admiral Hank the Zosha naval ship is on Dock 1, take your officers and greet them, show them around."

"Your majesty, before that," Duke Ridley bowed as he interrupted. Everyone froze waiting. The king nodded and Duke Ridley motioned to a servant who stepped forward with a chest, Ridley opened it and stated, "Our monarch would have loved to give these to you himself but did not want to wait for you to travel so far. Please accept these awards from Zosha's king, this is a medal never before given to foreign nationals however it is to show your bravery and dedication to your kingdom and allies while facing the unknown."

"It would be our honor, Duke Ridley," Hank stepped forward for it to be pinned on his chest. No one except the navy and his crew noticed he tugged his uniform slightly as a small motion of where to put it on the uniform since Ridley wasn't familiar with their uniforms. Saber waited for Mason to go then she stepped forward and then the rest. They saluted as the entire room cheered. Saber glanced at her family and followed the officers out to go to the docks. Hank scoffed softly seeing the ship before they even made it to the dock.

"What the hell?" Mason asked softly.

They went up the plank and Anthony popped up and welcomed them on board. "Navy crew?" Hank asked Axel and Dom who were smiling.

They were wearing uniforms but they looked comfortable and what any sailor would wear although they all matched. Saber was shocked. Dom explained they were royally pardoned so the wanted posters were a thing of the past. The king asked them to be a part of his navy and that he wanted to do this. After a while Hank asked if the officers wanted to go out to eat and Saber said, "Let's go to my house so we can talk in peace."

They all agreed and left. Twelve of them in two different uniforms. When they arrived the twins were excited to see the Zosha pirates and Ace stared in surprise to see them walking in the front door. Ulric and Giselle smiled seeing them all.

"So did the King say who was going to be the ambassador going with Captain York's crew?" Saber asked.

"For the first six months Marquis Gerard until a permanent ambassador can go," Giselle murmured.

"I'm thinking of volunteering," Ulric shocked everyone as they went to the dining room. Ace looked to Saber aware she was protective of the two.

"You can't just volunteer when Auntie isn't feeling well, Old Man!" she snarled at him.

"I actually mentioned wanting to see it," Giselle smiled at Saber who looked ready to go to war with Ulric, "The ingredients Red sent to me has made me feel better for over a year and that is just a tea from Zosha. What else is there that we don't know about?"

Saber studied her, "You are serious?"

"Yes, I want to see a different country, I've only ever known this country, Saber. Is that so surprising?"

Saber turned quiet and they changed the topic as they relaxed together. Saber slipped out to change her clothes since the other crew members had changed at the docks after seeing Axel's crew. When they were finished, Saber escorted them back to the ship talking to them some more. Dom asked her, "If Ulric and Giselle really become the ambassadors what will you do?"

"That's the question," Saber murmured as they got back on the ship, their crew watched her as Duke Ridley asked where they had been. Saber turned instantly to him and saluted as a naval officer to a noble, "Apologies sir, knowing the crew so well they were invited to my residence to have a meal with our officers. My parents, General

Thompson and Lady Giselle were interested in meeting them since they had heard so much of our adventure."

"I see," Ridley bowed slightly, "I am excited to witness the collaboration between your navy and our crew here."

"Captain Axel although there are still many things to go over as we discussed we usually do training in HQ at 0800, each crew gets an hour and we pair up to train. Vice Admiral Hank invited you but if you have preparations please feel free to use this to contact me and I can liaison between our crews. I'm the Combatant Commander so when we are on land I am second in command of the crew while Mason is second in command while at sea."

"Understood," Axel murmured, "I look forward to training with your crew."

"See you then," Saber agreed, "Duke Ridley I was to extend an invitation for you and the officers of Ax-Galley to supper one night this week to the Thompson Estate."

"Thank you, I will let the captain know which evenings are open as we have many things to settle this week."

"Of course," Saber agreed.

She left without a backward glance and Ridley noticed she was greeted by almost everyone on the wharf. "She said General Thompson and Lady Giselle?"

"Her parents," Axel nodded, "General Thompson is a war hero from his prime. He became a judge and traveled a lot. Lady Giselle is distantly related to the king in some capacity although I'm not sure how."

"But her last name is Barca?" Ridley frowned.

"Saber was adopted at the age of 14 although if you mention it to General Thompson or Lady Giselle they get very testy," Dom told Ridley seriously. Giselle turned quiet when Dom asked why they adopted Saber, thankfully Saber hadn't been home at the time just before they went to the unknown world. Ulric and Giselle made it clear that she was their daughter not 'adopted daughter'.

Saber and Axel were closer than ever and went nearly everywhere together when they were in port. Ulric had informed them that the king was very surprised he volunteered for the ambassador's position but Saber shocked them all when she said, "I want to stay with you both in Zosha then, I don't want to wait for every ship to take turns for six months there and wait for another turn and not get to see you for years on end."

"If Saber is going, we are going too," Ace murmured.

Ulric shook his head in surprise but told them they had a few months to talk about it. Saber had a date with Axel so left soon enough. Axel walked with her to the ambassador's house where Duke Ridley had invited him to dinner and to bring a plus one if he wanted. It was a small party for him to learn more of the nobles. Giselle and Ulric were attending but didn't know Saber was going with Axel. As they walked, Axel touched her elbow gently, "What's on your mind?"

"The Old Man said he volunteered to be ambassador and the king seemed favorable toward his request. I told him that if he was taking Auntie, I was going too but he said to think about it."

"If you went with your family, would you be able to stay in the navy?" Axel frowned.

"I'm not sure," Saber frowned.

"Don't get me wrong, I told you that you have a home there, Saber, I would love it for you to be there with me but you have a life here, friends and family here. I'm not just meaning Ulric and Giselle. What about Ace and the twins? Hank and the others?"

Saber loved the crew like family but she already didn't get to see her family enough because of work. She wished she could have everyone all together—Axel's crew and Hank's crew together, her family and all their families all in one spot so her heart didn't feel like it was being divided.

She sighed softly, "Sometimes I wish we were all from the same country so it isn't so far away."

Axel nodded, "Agreed."

They stepped in, Saber was in a dress which was a shock to the nobles that knew her well. They ate and danced before taking their leave. Duke Ridley was surprised to find Saber and Axel together but didn't say anything as they slipped out the door together.

Saber went to S-division to fill out paperwork and the head of S-Division said, "Heads up, Saber, the king plans to announce it tomorrow but Ulric Thompson will be the new ambassador and will travel with your crew to Zosha."

"Sir," she hesitated, "Lady Giselle isn't in great health and I don't get to see her often especially since it took over a year to travel the unknown world. I'm honestly wondering how I could stay in Zosha after the six months to be with my family. I don't really want to retire but at the same time I don't want Vice Admiral's crew to be forced to stay there either because I want to see my family more."

"Are you sure about this, Saber?" he frowned curiously.

"I feel like my heart will be in Zosha," she nodded.

"Let me talk to the Generals, with the Unknown world being opened up for exploration, it couldn't hurt to have another headquarters in Zosha for intelligence to flow from."

"Thank you sir," Saber nodded.

"Did you find your answer then?" he asked curiously.

"Is there more to life than fighting," Saber mused, "Yes I think I found my answer."

"What is it?" he asked wanting to know what she thought.

"Fighting is a tool to meet an end goal or need," she started, "You fight to protect what you love. That could be a nation, a loved one, a place.

Fighting isn't life it's a means to enjoy life and protect yourself and those you choose to protect."

"I'm glad you found your answer," he turned and headed toward the door, "I'll let you know if we need to have more discussions."

"Thank you sir," she murmured.

At the end of the day she had orders handed to her as a port wide announcement told that Giselle and Ulric were the ambassadors chosen to join the Zosha court. Her boss told her that a unit was going to protect them as the ambassadors and would be stationed there as well. They would rotate every six months along with the ships. Saber would have zero help although on each ship would be a S-division member to be trained by Saber while they were in port. Saber agreed to the orders. She went to the port, surprised that Ridley was there talking to the crew.

"Saber?" Axel asked forgetting to use her title. She fought a smile holding up her orders which stated she was to accompany the ambassadors as a naval representative. Axel stepped toward her and she let him read it. He stared at it in shock and Dom stepped closer, "What's up?"

"It's official," Saber ruffled Anthony's hair when he moved closer. Axel grinned looking down into her eyes, happy.

"Red doesn't have to worry about you trying to steal him away from the crew now," Axel murmured.

"True," Saber agreed.

"Someone tell me what's going on!" Dom frowned.

"You heard the announcement that my family is going to travel with our crew to be the official ambassadors right?" Saber asked him.

"Yes," Dom frowned.

"I got orders to be the naval representative to accompany them for their entire stay at Zosha. I'm going with Vice Admiral's crew to Zosha but when they leave...I stay."

"You stay...in Zosha for as long as General Thompson and Giselle stay as Ambassadors?" Dom asked curiously.

"Yes," she nodded, "There might be a few trips back here but I'm staying in Zosha."

Dom grabbed her and spun her with a laugh. She said, "Hank isn't happy about it but understands. He's taking up the merchants to Zosha every three months because it's better for his health he said so he's not going to go seven years without seeing you all."

"We celebrate tonight!" Axel announced, "Red make all Saber's favorites!"

"Aye!"

"I have to tell my family but I'll be back to celebrate," she murmured.

"Alright," he agreed.

She went home and gave her orders to her family, they were shocked but Ace pulled a letter out as well from the Army requesting him be a representative as well. They were all going to Zosha it seemed. She told them she'd be home late if at all, she was celebrating with the crew.

The six month training in Zosha as part of Hank's crew was great. Saber learned a lot. Ace and Saber also had work on top of that. Saber learned to dress for court and what that meant for Zosha. Axel and his crew were never gone long and were always there to help if they could. Within a year Axel and her got married. She was summoned to HQ for an in person report every year and Axel's crew took her there and back without much argument from their navy who knew Axel did mostly what he wanted.

When Ulric and Giselle truly retired, Axel and Saber became the ambassadors although Ace helped a lot since Saber married a native. They all lived in Zosha, the twins learned to fight from their family and learned the differences between the two countries, but also learned that fighting was a tool to keep those they loved safe, just as their aunt had learned. Saber became well known as the info broker and even helped

Zosha create their own intelligence network since a lot of islands and countries were against the Ruld-Zosha alliance.

Made in the USA
Middletown, DE
30 October 2023

41501286R00109